Love's Misbehaving Magic

Wildcrest Witches Book 3

HEATHER SILVIO

Panther Books

Panther Books: Worldwide.

Visit the author's website at https://www.heathersilvio.com
Contact the author at: heather@heathersilvio.com

Cover design by Sonia Freitas at Chloe Belle Arts
https://www.ChloeBelleArts.com

ISBN (Print) 978-1-951192-19-8
ISBN (E-book) 978-1-951192-20-4

BOOKS BY HEATHER SILVIO

WILDCREST WITCHES ROMANCE

Love's Misfiring Magic
Love's Misaligning Magic
Love's Misbehaving Magic

PARANORMAL TALENT AGENCY
(ALSO IN LARGE PRINT)

Lights, Camera, Action (Episode One)
Reset to One (Episode Two)
That's a Wrap (Episode Three)
An Unexpected Sequel (Episode Four)
Jumping the Shark (Episode Five)
The Season Finale (Episode Six)

COLLECTIONS

Paranormal Talent Agency Episodes 1-3 Collection
Paranormal Talent Agency Episodes 4-6 Collection
Paranormal Talent Agency Episodes 1-6 Collection

DOCTOR DANGER MYSTERIES

Hazard in Hawaii

NON-SERIES FICTION

Not Quite Famous: A Romantic Comedy of an Actress
on the Edge

Beyond the Abyss: Tales of the Supernatural

Courting Death

NONFICTION

Special Snowflake Syndrome: The Unrecognized
Personality Disorder Destroying the World

Happiness by the Numbers: 9 Steps to Authentic
Happiness

Stress Disorders: A Healing Path for PTSD

CHAPTER ONE

PATTY

Patricia Newsome hoped that once she walked through the teal double doors before her, she would find her personal, magical path. That lofty expectation explained the butterflies swarming inside her. Time for action. She raised her hand to rap on the door with her knuckles. Except the door swung open, and a body came barreling out.

"Oof, excuse me," Patricia mumbled into the shoulder of the person who had just crashed into her. The tall, well-built someone who smelled amazing, with a clean, bright herbal scent. "I was about to knock," she explained as she lifted her gaze and saw longish brown hair framing dark brown eyes. "Noah! What are you doing here?"

The skin around Noah Wright's eyes crinkled with a smile. "Hi Patty, sorry about that. I didn't see you there."

She laughed and lifted one shoulder in a shrug. "Wouldn't be the first time, given that I'm, ahem, height-challenged." Unlike Noah, who was the very definition of a tall drink of water.

Noah stepped through the front door of his parents' home and held it open for her. "I was just leaving. Are you here to see my mother or my father?"

"Your father, if he's available."

"I believe he's out back. Do you want me to get him for you?"

"Nah, that's not necessary. I'll head around the side." She stepped away from the open door, and Noah followed. Curious. And a bit intriguing.

"How's school?" he asked, shifting his green backpack from one shoulder to the other.

"Great. I can't believe I'm graduating with my master's degree in only one more semester." She shook her head.

"In Theology, right?"

"You remembered."

Noah winked. "My excellent tutoring clearly helped you get there."

"No doubt, my improved algebra skills made all the difference when studying alternative religions," Patty responded deadpan.

"No doubt," he agreed with a solemn nod.

They stood in silence for a beat, and she wondered if she was imagining the spark she felt between them. Patty had always found him attractive. Especially in high school, when he was her older tutor – high school senior to her freshman. But she hadn't seen him until this summer when she'd made her discovery about his mother.

"How's your mother?" she asked, and his face grew troubled. All the witches in Wildcrest, Nevada had a magical inclination, and Noah's was healing abilities. He might look like the stereotype of a cowboy in his flannel shirts, jeans, and brown boots. But, no, he was Wildcrest's only family doctor who made house calls.

He ran a hand through his longish brown hair. "The same," he answered in a lowered voice. "Ben tried to read her, to find what might be wrong with her. He couldn't tell, so I tried a general healing spell. It didn't seem to do anything."

"Have you spoken to Esther about it?"

Noah flushed.

"That would be a no, then," she teased.

"We've seen the impact of whatever is going on with Mom," Noah said. "But since you're the only one who has actually seen something wrong with her, we're not sure how to approach it. My brothers and your sister have said we need to meet to discuss what to do, but we don't."

"Avoiding?"

Noah nodded.

"Is that a good idea?" Patty scanned his face, took in the worry lines and troubled expression marring the chiseled cheekbones. She knew she'd upended the family during their last Wiccan celebration when she had been shocked to witness Esther Wright's magical aura.

All witches had magical energy radiating from them like an aura. Patty's gift was to see and interpret those magical auras. Except that for as long as she had known Esther Wright, though the woman might be a brilliant and beautiful person, she was not a witch. Esther never had a magical aura. Only apparently, now she did and therefore she was a witch. There was no other explanation for why Esther would have a magical aura. And her developing magic was interfering with other witches' magic. It was a bizarre scenario none of them had encountered before. Patty had researched it when she returned to school after the celebration, but found no recorded instances of a person developing magical abilities outside of puberty.

"How do you tell your mother she's not only a witch, but possibly a broken one?" Noah crossed and uncrossed his arms. "Have you seen anything else?"

"No, I haven't. Maybe we should have a meeting with her?" Patty suggested.

Noah looked uncomfortable, though gave a curt nod.

"How's work?" Patty asked instead, hoping it would be a safer topic, though she made a mental note to speak to his brothers.

Noah's relieved expression reinforced Patty's decision to change the topic. "It's great. This morning, I healed a small femur fracture that happened when a goat tripped and fell on its owner."

"A goat? No!" Patty exclaimed.

"Yep."

"Is the goat okay?"

"Yes," he responded, and they shared another smile.

A moment before the silence grew uncomfortable, a booming voice sounded from the back of the home.

"Who's at the door, son?"

"It's Patty," Noah called over his shoulder to his father, his eyes never leaving Patty's.

She grew warm under the scrutiny. "I'd like to talk to you about a job after graduation," she hollered from the front doorway to Elijah Wright, the coven's high priest, who likely was in the kitchen on the other end of the large home.

She couldn't miss the bright flare of Noah's typically muted pink aura to a brighter, richer pink, with her explanation of why she was on his parents' doorstep. The flare threw her for a moment.

To respect other witches' emotional privacy, she tried not to read their auras without their permission; except sometimes when their emotions sparked, their auras were unavoidable.

Noah's bright, rich pink aura suggested attraction. She'd thought she'd seen a hint of it at the celebration earlier in the summer, and again when he opened the door. But it definitely flared brighter just now. And if he could read magical auras, hers no doubt would match.

CHAPTER TWO

NOAH

The rush of pleasure when Patty stated her intention with his father surprised Noah. Because that meant she wanted to move back to town after graduation? That wasn't surprising. Most witches returned to Wildcrest. After all, who wouldn't want to live relatively openly among other supernatural beings, chiefly witches, if they had the opportunity to do so? His father's continued speech stopped Noah's rush of thoughts.

"A job?" Elijah hollered, his booming voice easily traveling from the kitchen to the front door where Noah and Patty still stood.

"Yes, sir," Patty hollered back and then winked at Noah.

He caught himself before he winked back. That wasn't an appropriate response, he didn't think. She was staring at him, waiting for him to… oh right. "I guess you don't need to go around the side of the house," Noah said, stepping back through the doorway into the foyer.

"Kitchen?" she asked him, pointing as if they both didn't know the way by heart. They'd spent hours in the kitchen together when he tutored her.

"Kitchen," he answered, and then closed the door behind her. She wore jeans, a t-shirt, and turquoise Converse, which he swore she wore almost exclusively during high school. "Nice Chucks."

She glanced at him over her shoulder and gave him a coquettish wave. Then she kicked up one foot, but didn't say anything.

Noah laughed and continued to follow the tiny woman through the foyer, her shoes silent on the terracotta tile flooring, in contrast to the clacking of his boots.

He stopped in the doorway to the kitchen. Patty was embracing his parents.

"Elijah," she said, wrapping her arms around the burly man, her head not reaching his shoulders.

"It's great to see you," Elijah said. "I'm sorry we didn't get a chance to chat much at the celebration."

Patty waved away the apology, disentangled herself from his father's hug, and hugged his mother. "How are you doing, Esther?"

Noah understood the subtext to that question, but he doubted his parents did. And, judging from his mother's response, she definitely didn't pick up on anything other than a social nicety in the greeting.

"I'm great, Patty. I'll echo my husband. It's great to see you." Esther sat at the white oak table, gesturing for Patty and the men to do the same. "Did I hear right? Are you here about a job?"

Patty glanced around the table at Elijah, Esther, and Noah, then bit her lower lip.

"Hadn't planned on a whole crowd, had you?" Noah teased and she gave a bobble-headed nod. "We can leave."

"Oh," Esther said, "of course. You're like family. It never even occurred to me." She lifted her hand like she wanted to run it through her hair, but forgot she had done her French braid.

"Let's go, Mom," Noah said to Esther, before mouthing *good luck* to Patty. She mouthed *thank you* and visibly relaxed.

Patty and Noah stood. "I can't wait to catch up after we're finished," Patty offered, as Noah led his mother back out of the kitchen and onto the deck.

The two sat on wooden deck chairs situated to overlook the Nevada desert beyond the property. It was still early afternoon, so the sun blazed in a cloudless blue sky. Its rays warmed the brown and green scrub brush surrounding the home.

Noah sank his tall frame into the chair and breathed in the fresh air.

"Do you know what job Patty's asking your father about?" Esther whispered the words, though Noah doubted that Patty or Elijah could hear inside the house.

Nevertheless, he matched her tone and volume. He even leaned closer. "I don't. Her degree is in theology, so it might have something to do with Dad as the high priest of the coven." He cocked his head. "Is that Richard?"

Esther and Noah peered at the scrub brush off to the side of the deck. A gray wolf appeared and sauntered over to them, stopping between their two deck chairs.

Noah scratched the wolf behind the ears and was rewarded with a tail thump of pleasure. "How are you doing, Richard?"

The wolf's tongue lolled out in response and Esther chuckled. "Elijah is inside," she said to her husband's familiar.

Noah didn't think the wolf fully understood his mother, but the wolf certainly understood his father's name. Richard – a Wright warrior ancestor from several hundred years ago – settled between the chairs and rested his head on outstretched paws.

"Did I sense something between you and Patty?" Esther asked her son.

Noah's eyebrows practically jumped off his forehead before he recovered. But not fast enough.

"I did," she answered her own question.

"She's like my little sister," he blurted out in response, his face flushing. His reaction to Patty continued to *not* feel like family-member feelings.

"Uh-huh." His mother leaned back in the chair, eyes closed, lifting her face to the sun.

Noah mimicked her, enjoying the gentle breeze on his skin, and wondered about his mixed reactions to Patty. He'd always thought she was cute, but in a platonic way. Like a little sister. Except, that rush of pleasure when she'd said she was asking his father about a job… that wasn't like the pleasure of reuniting with a family member. Not at all. The thought of seeing her every day, or spending time with her… he never felt like that when he thought about seeing his brothers, that was certain.

He found himself wondering if she'd experienced something similar.

CHAPTER THREE

PATTY

Patty hadn't realized how much the clashing auras in the kitchen upset her magical balance until Esther and Noah left the room. It hadn't just been Noah's aura, suggesting an interest in her. Esther's aura continued to swirl a chaotic mix of colors, and for the first time, worry appeared in Elijah's aura. Patty sighed in relief with their exit.

"Is that sigh about me?" Elijah teased.

Her face reddened and she sat across from him at the kitchen table. "Not at all," she said, though that wasn't entirely accurate.

Did he sense something with Esther, or was it unrelated? She wasn't comfortable asking him, since he wasn't aware his aura was flashing like this, so she cleared her throat and focused on her reason for the visit.

"As you know," she began, her hands rubbing the smooth oak top before she caught herself, "I'm graduating with my Master of Arts in Theological Studies at the end of the upcoming semester."

"Congratulations in advance," he interrupted her.

"Thank you," she accepted with a grin. "The next step in my career is to secure employment." She breathed deeply, the scent of the Wright's coffee calming her. "And I'd like that job to be with Wildcrest Witches International."

"Tell me what role you'd like to fill," Elijah said. "We don't have any openings."

Butterflies returned at the comment, but she wasn't surprised. "I can appreciate that," she said with a nod. The coven's business was a small one, and she'd need to make the case for herself. "I have an idea for a new role, one that would combine my Wiccan knowledge with business acumen."

"I'm listening," he said, leaning back in the chair, his arms resting on the white oak table, brown eyes reflecting curiosity.

Patty paused before launching into a summary of her ideas. She recommended creating an online version of their coven. That would allow the company to grow beyond the local activities they currently focused on, without sacrificing their in-person activities. "We could even have retreats for witches who want to experience in-person celebrations."

Elijah frowned.

Worry spiked that he wouldn't accept her ideas. "It would never be at the expense of our town members, of course," she rushed to reassure him. "But it would offer solitary practitioners in the supernatural world the support they might not otherwise get." His nod emboldened her. "It would also allow me the opportunity to learn from you and…" She swallowed as she mentally tripped at admitting her true ambition aloud.

"And?"

"Become the high priestess myself one day." Her eyes widened as she waited for his reaction.

Elijah tilted his head, taking her in.

She tried not to fidget under his gaze. This was a big plan for the future and he was the first person she'd shared it with. What if he hated her aspiration? Her breath caught in her throat.

"That's intriguing," he finally said.

She whooshed out the breath she was holding.

He chuckled. "Diversifying sources of income, growing the company without sacrificing our local witches," he processed what she'd offered. "And become the high priestess when I retire. Intriguing indeed."

Patty had considered her pitch a lot. She didn't believe any of the Wright sons were interested in becoming the high priest, and although it wouldn't be soon, Elijah would eventually step down. She believed in her heart that she would be a great coven leader. Her natural empathy for others combined with her magical inclination and the information she was learning in graduate school seemed like the perfect trifecta. At least to her.

"Let me think about it," Elijah said, holding out his hand, which she took. "I'll let you know." Elijah's magenta aura pulsed brighter, unavoidable, but the powerful color, consistent with his strong-willed originality, suggested the idea indeed intrigued him.

Patty relaxed further at the unexpected sight. "Thank you." She stood from the chair. "I appreciate the consideration."

Elijah walked her out, and her heart jumped when she saw Noah sitting in his truck in the driveway. His head down indicated he was reviewing a patient chart or was on his phone. She crossed the stone paver driveway to knock on his window.

He startled, then relaxed when he saw it was her. The window lowered.

Although unable to explain why the Wrights' auras seemed conspicuous today, Noah's bright pink shining aura of happiness in seeing her bolstered her nerves and she boldly opened with, "Hey good-looking."

CHAPTER FOUR

NOAH

Did she just greet me with hey good-looking? Noah stammered something unintelligible in response and waited for her follow-up, while he berated himself for missing an opportunity. Wait, did that mean he wanted to flirt?

Her expression fell, and a frisson of guilt surfaced. She surely was joking around, and he took it too seriously, and maybe hurt her feelings.

"How did it go with my dad?" he asked, choosing the path of ignoring the discomfort.

Patty accepted the side-stepping. "It went well. I offered my ideas for a job and he said it was intriguing."

He wondered about specifics, but figured she'd share when she was ready. "You staying in town is definitely intriguing," he said, echoing his father's response. Again, a flash of pleasure surged through him at the idea of her staying in Wildcrest after graduation. That needed to stop. They were just friends.

"Thank you." Patty frowned and bit her lower lip. "I'm still concerned about Esther."

At Patty's expression of concern, Noah's worry about his mother heightened. "Did you see something new today?"

She hesitated. "Not new, exactly, but there appeared to be an increase in the intensity of the chaos in your mother's magical aura."

"An aura that she shouldn't even have."

"That we wouldn't expect her to have," Patty gently corrected. "Shouldn't is a strong word."

"Touché," he said, inclining his head.

"Certainly, since as far as we knew, she never had any magic, the presence of a magical aura is unexpected." She placed her hands on her hips.

He smothered a smile. She'd adopted that superhero stance as a kid and used it whenever she was thinking. Noah wondered if she was aware of that.

"The intensity increase within her new aura concerns me, though. Especially since we don't understand what any of this means."

"It might be a good thing?"

"An increase in chaos is rarely a good thing, but, honestly, I just don't know." Patty nibbled on her lower lip again, and heat suffused his face. He hoped she missed it.

Noah closed his eyes for a moment. Patty's comment from earlier was accurate. They needed to call a family meeting to discuss his mother's… condition? He didn't know what to call it.

"Noah?"

His eyes popped back open. "Apologies. I was considering our options."

"And?"

"You're right—"

"Of course," she interrupted with a wink.

He chuckled, then sobered. "We need to meet as a family to discuss what this might mean."

Patty reached up to place one hand on his arm where he leaned out his open window. "I think you should include your parents."

The feel of her fingers against his skin distracted him.

"It's about Esther, so she should be there," she added in a stronger tone.

Patty's tone broke the spell of her distraction. "I'm not disagreeing with you."

"Oh, when you stayed quiet…"

"I was distracted." Both their gazes landed on his arm, where her hand still lingered.

She snatched it back. "Ah, I see."

He wished she'd put her hand back on his arm.

"You know," Patty said, her voice taking on an unfamiliar slinky sound. "We could go out sometime."

"Like on a date?" he stammered. "I don't know."

"I'm only here until the end of the month," she backtracked.

"So not a date?"

She shook her head, appearing confused. "I'm not a big label person. But we could call it a summer fling." She hooked a come-hither finger at him. "I hear those are popular."

He opened and closed his mouth like a fish, unable to find his voice.

"It's not a trick question," she teased, leaning against the truck.

A scent of vanilla wafted around him. That had been her signature scent since high school. Right then, it made him hungry. "I'm not interested in you," he said instead.

"Your aura would suggest otherwise."

"That's unfair," he grumbled, though her observing his aura uninvited surprised him. A smidge of irritation bubbled. That wasn't like her to read auras without permission.

"Life isn't fair," she responded cheerfully, and he couldn't help but laugh. "And just so you know, I'm not trying to see your aura. Your family is very… visible today."

"Thanks for explaining." He broke eye contact, now feeling bad about his unwarranted irritation. Of course, she wouldn't purposefully read his aura without permission. "I'm still not having a fling with you."

"You're so caught up in labels," she joked, though he thought he heard the disappointment underneath.

Or was he confusing her tone with his own disappointment that all she wanted was a fling?

CHAPTER FIVE

PATTY

With Noah's reaction, Patty wanted to eat her words. She was so convinced he'd say yes – his aura told her that he found her attractive – it hadn't occurred to her that he wouldn't. She tamped down the surge of disappointment and backpedaled.

"No worries," she sang out with false bravado. "It was just an impulsive question."

"I hope you know it isn't—"

"Personal? Of course, I know that," she interrupted and waved off his explanation. Her hurt feelings could be dealt with later. This would only get more and more awkward if she didn't cut it off. Now. She made a show of glancing at his watch, as if they both had more important places to be. "It was great seeing you, as always." She turned to walk away, then stopped. "Though if you'd like me to come to the family meeting about Esther." She bit her lower lip. "I'm not family—"

This time, he cut her off. "You're family," he disagreed.

Her pressured thoughts to flee the uncomfortable conversation settled at the finality with which he made the statement. "Thanks," she whispered. "My job suggestion to your father was to assist him with his high priest duties, so that I can be the high priestess one day."

Noah's jaw dropped open at the blurted statement.

But, she found this time she didn't regret the impromptu detail. The comfort she'd felt in the conversation led her to believe he would support the idea. Support *her*, if she was honest with herself.

"That's a wonderful idea," he said. "You'd make a great high priestess when my father steps down."

A shy smile played at her lips. She'd hoped for his support, but actually receiving it – and immediately, no less – flooded her with warmth. "Thank you, Noah."

"Of course," he said, and they shared a heated glance. "As for Mom, I'll let you know what we schedule." This time, he glanced at his watch. "I really do have to go, though."

"Have a good day," she said with a half-wave, glad the awkwardness had abated somewhat. Albeit not fully.

She walked to her vehicle, the sound of his truck starting and pulling away a mixed soundtrack to her walk of shame.

Patty mentally smacked herself. It wasn't a walk of shame. No need to exaggerate. She asked him out and he said no. They were both adults. It could disappoint her without embarrassing her.

Driving back to her parents' house in her bright red hatchback, she kept the windows lowered to enjoy the late summer breezes and sang along to the radio. She gave her brain time to process what she'd said, done, and learned that morning at the Wright house.

An idea percolated to the top as she pulled into her parents' driveway.

A deep bark greeted her when she opened the door to the sprawling ranch-style home. She entered the foyer and kneeled down to love on the Great Dane before her.

"Hey Max," she said, running her fingers along his black face and down his tan body. He wiggled his butt in appreciation, before heading back the way he'd probably come. Maximillian, better known as Max, was her father's familiar. Max was reticent about where in the family tree he resided, and Patty assumed it would remain one of life's great mysteries.

Sort of like her own familiar, she thought, as she headed toward her childhood bedroom. Like all the women in her family, she too had a less common familiar. No cats or dogs for any of them. "Hi Aveline," she greeted the sandy brown desert owl whose ancestor spirit was so ancient the source seemed lost to time.

"Welcome back," Aveline hooted. The shy owl rarely left Patty's room during the day, though enjoyed touring the desert surrounding Wildcrest at night.

"Let me run something by you," Patty said to the owl before laying back on the yellow bedspread of the unmade bed.

"Proceed," Aveline hooted.

Patty caught her familiar up on the proposal to Elijah Wright and the continued chaotic magic in Esther's aura. She swallowed, reminded herself that there was no reason to be embarrassed, and then shared how Noah shot down her invitation.

"A summer fling?"

"Is that disdain in your voice, Ave?"

"That's not really like you, and it's definitely not like Noah."

A flush crept up Patty's neck. "What was I thinking?"

"You weren't."

Patty chuckled. "Isn't that the truth?"

"What are you going to do?"

"I don't know," Patty admitted, staring at the ceiling, waiting for inspiration. Her prior idea continued percolating. She considered the connections between the personal and professional issues with her and the members of the Wright family. Perhaps she could kill two birds with one stone.

Ugh, that's a horrible saying. Patty shot a glance at her owl, glad the familiar couldn't read her mind.

She bolted up. "I think I have a plan."

"This isn't anything harebrained like your sister's plan was?"

Patty's older sister, Shelly, had played with magic to convince an ex-boyfriend to reunite with her, with the expected disastrous results. Although, in the end, Shelly figured out where her heart was, and she'd gotten her happily ever after.

Noah's face flashed in her mind, and Patty startled. She was interested in Noah, sure, but he wasn't her happily ever after.

Was he? They both prioritized family, valued professionalism, and enjoyed what life offered. Plus, they had a healthy dose of attraction between them.

Why couldn't he be her happily ever after?

Oh, yeah, because that's not what he wanted.

"Patty? Your plan?" The owl interrupted Patty's rapid thoughts.

"Yes. My plan!" She inhaled. "There are several overlapping areas in my life right now," she said both to Aveline and herself as she worked this out in her mind. "I want Noah to look at me like more than a little sister – and act on it," she clarified. Relief surged that she could acknowledge to herself that she did, in fact, want him.

She frowned. "I want to help Esther in whatever way I can, to help her understand and develop whatever type of magic she now has."

"Finally, I want Elijah to agree to my proposal to expand the online footprint of Wildcrest Witches International, with a long-term goal of me becoming the high priestess."

"Excellent summary," Aveline hooted and Patty swore she saw laughter in the owl's yellow eyes.

"Thank you," Patty said, accepting the praise at face value. She leapt from the bed and spun to face the owl, who perched on a large tree in the room's corner.

"So, this is my plan. I'll offer to help Esther, which will hopefully actually help her. That help will show Elijah what I'd bring to the coven in an official capacity. Last but not least," she said with a grin, "I'll use the proximity to Noah to convince him we should at least go out on a date."

Aveline's hooting response was unmistakably laughter this time, though the owl offered her support. "If anyone can do it, you can."

"All before I leave for my last semester of school at the end of the month. Easy peasy." She nibbled on her lower lip. "First step. Figure out what the heck is going on with Esther and her unexpected magic."

CHAPTER SIX

NOAH

Wildcrest Wizardry was one of his favorite places in town. Between the delectable scents from the coffee shop side of the business and the incredible array of herbs on the apothecary side, he loved that it represented the notion of helping. Each aisle of the apothecary focused on a different area of magic. Right now, he needed additional herbs to supplement his magical healing for his next house call.

"Can I help you find anything, Noah?" Rebekah, the tall, blonde manager of the store, asked him. "Probably not," she answered herself, "but I figured there's no harm in asking. I suspect you know even better than I do where everything is."

He joined in her easy laughter. "I'm good, thank you."

"Tell me if you change your mind," she said and then hurried to the front station to check out a customer.

Noah frowned as he considered his options. He needed peppermint, ginger, and stinging nettle to address Bobby's damaged lungs.

The scent of vanilla reached him before he heard her voice.

"Let's turn that frown upside down," Patty said in an unusual, lilting cadence.

He placed the last of his selected herbs in the handheld cart and offered her a smirk. "How do you plan to do that?"

"Depends on the source of the frown."

"It's for a patient."

"Ah, a little natural magic booster."

"Precisely." Although his magical inclination was to heal others, it wasn't that cut and dried. With some illnesses and injuries, the healing was like a movie. He'd hover his hands over the problematic body part, and they'd get better.

His younger brother, Ben, had asked him about the process when Ben's ability to recognize what a sick person needed, whether physical or magical, first developed. Their parents had said that it wasn't uncommon for siblings to develop similar magical abilities like that.

Noah had explained that when he healed someone, his fingertips tingled. With practice, he'd learned that when those tingles turned painful, that was the Goddess telling him that his magic alone wasn't sufficient to heal the person's illness or injury.

When his magic wasn't sufficient, he turned to other magical enhancement, whether crystals, herbs, or intentional spell work. Except in the most advanced cases, between his own magic and the magical enhancements, he succeeded. In only a year, he had built up a thriving house call service. He enjoyed helping individuals who wouldn't otherwise be able or willing to seek help outside their homes.

Patty knew all of that, too. They'd had many conversations about his medical intentions during their tutoring sessions. He remembered her, as always, so supportive of his plans.

"Do you expect it to be enough?" she asked now, and he understood she was curious, not questioning his abilities.

"I believe so," he replied. The patient's illness had progressed further than Noah would have liked. He wished Bobby had contacted him sooner. But Noah had healed similar issues before, so he remained optimistic.

She placed her hands on her hips.

"What?" he asked, an unfamiliar emotion fluttering through him, feeling heavy in his chest. He wondered about its origins, before focusing on Patty instead. "Lay it on me."

"Can I come with you?"

His eyebrows rose. "To see my patient?"

"Yes."

He couldn't imagine a reason she'd want to. "For what reason?"

"I have an idea to help your mother, and it'll give us the ride out to the house to discuss it."

The explanation, and shift from his patient to his mother, startled him. "How do you know the drive will be long enough?"

"Educated guess. I don't believe many of your clients are close to town."

"You're not wrong," he agreed, a thrill surging that she'd thought about his practice. "Is there a reason you can't explain the idea to me now?" He asked for curiosity's sake, since he'd already decided to say yes.

She scuffed sandals on the floor, not meeting his eyes.

That confirmed she had an ulterior motive.

"I don't want to hold you up," she explained.

A perfectly reasonable explanation. And yet. He knew her. There was something more. Could it have something to do with her asking him out before? He'd already told her no, so surely she wouldn't ask again. He ignored that as a possible explanation.

She watched him consider her request; he hoped his aura wasn't flashing again.

"I'll text the patient, and if he's not okay with you coming inside, you'll have to wait in the car," he warned her, his already baritone voice deepening.

"Understood."

He pulled his phone from the front pocket of his jeans to text Bobby. Noah emphasized that Patty needed to talk to Noah during the drive, and could wait in the truck at the house. He read the response and then lifted his gaze, his brown eyes finding her hazel ones.

"It must be your lucky day. He said it's too hot for you to wait in the car, regardless of the existence of air conditioning."

"Aw, that's sweet." She touched his arm. "But I don't want to be an imposition, or to make him feel uncomfortable."

He enjoyed the touch of her hand on his elbow for the briefest of moments before responding. "Believe me, if he didn't want you there, he would have said no. This is not someone who has a hard time speaking his mind."

"As long as you're sure."

"I am. Let's do it." He'd just try to figure out her ulterior motive while they drove.

CHAPTER SEVEN

PATTY

The mapping software informed her she had twenty minutes to lay out her plan before they reached Noah's patient's home. That would be plenty of time.

"While we don't understand the *why* or *how* of what's happening with your mother, the existence of a magical aura tells me she has magic. Period," Patty bluntly began.

"Agreed."

"So, I envision a multi-step plan."

Noah chuckled. "You do, huh?"

She gave him the side-eye, which only made him laugh harder. "I do."

"Please enlighten me." His fingers on the steering wheel tapped along with the radio playing softly in the background.

"Step one is to talk to your mother." Patty remained shocked the Wright men hadn't broached the topic. That needed to be rectified as soon as possible.

"How would you recommend we approach her?"

"Matter of fact. With me present, ideally."

"Ideally?"

"Yes. Probably Laura too."

Noah nodded as he took the highway entrance ramp. "That makes sense."

"I can explain that I see a magical aura, and Laura can explain how Esther's proximity to her has made her magic wonky."

"Wonky?"

"To use the technical term," Patty explained with a wink.

"Please continue," Noah said with a theatrical wave.

"Your mother is smart—"

"Thanks," he interrupted.

"—and I think that will be enough for her to accept that something is happening. Plus, then we can ask—" Patty side-eyed Noah again. "—your mother how she's been feeling. There's a very good chance that she can tell something is happening."

Noah's eyebrows rose. "Do you think she knows she's got magic?"

"I don't know." Patty lifted a single shoulder. "But I find it highly unlikely that she has enough magic for me to see a magic aura AND for it to interfere with Laura's magic, without Esther feeling something."

"Makes sense," Noah said again. He exited the highway and hung a sharp right onto a dirt road. "Step two?"

"Step two," Patty began, "is to help your mother learn to manipulate the magical energy she has."

"How exactly are you going to do that?"

She fiddled with the A/C vent, angling it toward her and then off her face again. "That's the tricky part," she admitted.

"No doubt," he said as he pulled up to a small, squat, but well-kept beige stucco house.

"Once we have a better understanding of how the magic feels to Esther, then we can work with her. I can watch how the chaos in her aura responds to anything that we do. My assumption is that as she learns how to control her magic, the chaos in her aura will decrease."

Noah turned the truck off and twisted in his seat. Patty read the uncertainty on his face.

"Trust me," she urged him. "It'll work."

"I don't know," he said and turned away to exit the car. Patty scrambled to do the same, anxiety spiking that her plan might be finished before it even started. When she met him at the front of the truck, she grabbed his elbow.

"What's the worst that can happen?"

His gaze dropped to her hand on his arm, but this time, his expression remained unreadable.

She spread her arms wide. "It's our best bet right now. Do you have a better idea?"

"No, I don't. But." He sighed. "I'm just not comfortable experimenting on my mother."

Before Patty could argue with him that her plan wasn't experimenting, the door to the home opened and an older man stood in the doorway.

"I'll check with my brothers after the visit, but the answer will probably be no," Noah said with finality. He strode away from her, hand extended. "Bobby."

"Hey, doc," the older man responded in a raspy voice. "This is your friend?" Bobby asked as he peered beyond Noah at Patty, who'd remained a few feet back.

At the question, she also strode forward, hand extended. "Hi, Bobby, I'm Patty," she said, startled by his weak handshake. "Thank you for allowing me to accompany Noah." She gazed up at Bobby's wrinkled face surrounded by wispy, gray hair, and he offered a lop-sided smile. Stained teeth combined with his raspy voice suggested a probable source of his illness.

"Nice to meet you," Bobby said, before indicating the two should follow him inside.

The faint scent of tobacco confirmed Patty's guesses about his illness; lung cancer or emphysema, she wondered.

Bobby hitched up the pants falling off his narrow hipbones and collapsed onto the faded corduroy couch.

When Noah took the spot next to him, Patty scooted over to a blue rocking chair and perched on the edge.

"How are you feeling today?" Noah asked Bobby.

The older man knelt over as a coughing fit overwhelmed him. Patty's heart broke to see the suffering, and she hoped Noah's abilities weren't overstated. She recognized it was silly superstition, but she crossed her fingers behind her bag in a quick wish to the Goddess.

"Sorry 'bout that," Bobby said when the fit subsided. "Emphysema," he explained to Patty, and she nodded. "Quit smoking, but, eh, the damage's been done."

"Are you ready?" Noah asked, and Bobby nodded.

Patty realized with a start that they were jumping right into the healing. Noah had obviously already done a preliminary visit. Despite their shared history, she'd never seen him heal someone.

Noah placed a ceramic mortar on the glass top of the coffee table before them and filled it with the herbs he'd bought at the apothecary earlier.

Patty and Bobby remained quiet, absorbed in Noah's process.

Noah crushed the peppermint, ginger, and stinging nettle with the ceramic pestle, muttering under his breath.

Patty strained to hear the words, but they stayed unintelligible; however, she couldn't miss his aura. It blazed with shades of green, blue, and a light teal. All the colors associated with healing.

"This part will be quick," Noah assured Bobby, before lighting the mixture on fire.

The sweet scents of peppermint and ginger filled the small space. This was why Noah had left Bobby's front door open, Patty realized. With a final few words of the incantation, Noah blew out the flame. Embers continued to glow. Noah faced Bobby, who closed his eyes without being instructed to do so.

Patty sat transfixed while Noah's hands roamed maybe an inch or two over the older man's body. Noah's hands slowed and halted over Bobby's chest. She caught her breath when an aura sputtered around Bobby. Noah's healthy aura grew darker as Bobby's strengthened, then both auras mixed, before separating and brightening. Noah's returned to a healing light blue and green, and Bobby's settled at a warm orange. That social and thoughtful color fit with Bobby inviting her to stay for his healing.

Bobby inhaled deeply and a wide grin broke out over his weathered face. "I haven't been able to do that in… I don't know how long," he admitted.

"We'll get you in for some testing to confirm, but I believe you're good to go," Noah said, his voice bearing a hint of exhaustion to Patty's ears. He provided detailed follow-up information, and the two exchanged their goodbyes.

Watching Noah heal Bobby had been exhilarating for Patty. All magic was amazing, a gift from the Goddess. But, something about Noah's healing moved her in a way other witch's magic hadn't. Could that be connected to her attraction to him?

Patty rose to her feet when the men did, caught by surprise, as she was still reviewing in her mind what she'd witnessed. Noah's healing abilities impressed her tremendously. His medical background combined with his magical abilities made a potent combination. His ability to work directly with a witch's aura to aid their healing was nothing short of miraculous.

Now that she understood more about how those abilities worked, she had an idea to convince him to partner with her to help his mother.

CHAPTER EIGHT

NOAH

Gratification and exhaustion coexisted in Noah after the healing. He understood he had a gift, and he received immense pleasure in helping his fellow witches. It was also tremendously exhausting work. A trickle of unease filtered in, wondering what Patty thought of what she'd witnessed.

"What did you think?" Noah asked Patty once they were seated back in his truck for the return to town. For obvious reasons, other than family members of his patients, he'd never had someone watch him work like that before. The small surge of anxiety suggested he wanted her to be impressed. That seemed odd to him.

"That was amazing," she gushed, and pride washed over Noah. "I've never seen anything like that before."

"I imagine you don't follow doctors around much," he joked.

"True," she said with a laugh, "but that's not what I meant."

He glanced at her. "What do you mean?" She met his gaze for a moment before his eyes returned to the road.

"I could see you heal him."

"Well, yes, you were right there as I combined my abilities with the spell." He heard the confusion in his tone.

"No, I mean, I saw his aura change as you healed him," she explained.

"Oh." His mind swirled with that knowledge. "What did that look like?"

Patty walked him through what she'd seen, and his mind continued to swirl in the background as she did so.

"Bobby's magic really suffered during his illness," Noah said when she finished.

She nodded. "I wondered. The way it sputtered, but then grew in strength." Now she shook her head. "That was just so amazing," she repeated.

"I'd never realized my magic mixed with theirs so specifically," he admitted. "Knowing his magic seems to have recovered along with his physical self, right there during treatment..." Noah trailed off. "We make a good team."

"Yes, we do," she agreed. She placed her hand on his, resting on the stick shift. The softness of her skin and the naturalness of the movement caught him. He wanted more of it. More of Patty. "And I think I know how to help your mother."

He opened his mouth to remind her he was going to speak to his brothers, but she removed her hand from his and barreled forward.

"If we partner on this, we'll be that much more effective."

Noah remained quiet; his mind had taken him down a similar road. He wondered if they'd ended up at the same conclusion.

"The way your aura mixed with Bobby's suggests perhaps the same would happen with Esther. You can use your healing powers – and the interaction of your aura – to help stabilize hers, while I guide her verbally." Patty spoke as if working through the plan while she uttered the words. She spun in her seat to face him. "What do you think?"

He cut his eyes to hers before returning them to the road. "I think you've convinced me," he admitted.

"You don't need to run it by Ben and Aaron?" she teased.

"No, I don't." He smiled. "Though, of course, it'll be my mom's call."

"Naturally. I'd never try to work magic on someone without their knowledge."

She sounded so indignant he couldn't help but probe. "Unlike our siblings?" His brother and her sister had made some poor choices together earlier in the year, though everything ended well.

"Exactly," she agreed.

Her silence after the emphatic agreement surprised him, and he glanced at her again. She wore an odd expression; when she caught him looking, it changed into something lighthearted, but slyer. A chuckle threatened to erupt; he loved how she brought out such joy in him with her exuberance and playful scheming. She leaned closer, her vanilla scent brushed against him, tantalizing.

"Yes?" he asked.

"Since we make such a great team—"

"Are you sure you want to go there?" he interrupted her, clearing his throat to cover the sudden dryness.

"You'll go out with me then?" she continued as if he hadn't interrupted.

"I'm not dating my brother's girlfriend's baby sister," he blurted out.

"Exactly."

"Huh?" he responded not-so-eloquently to her unexpected rejoinder.

"You wouldn't be dating your brother's girlfriend's baby sister," she agreed with him.

Noah laughed. "Now I'm just confused. Are you asking me out again or not?"

"Yes, I am."

He cut his eyes at her again. "Explain."

"I'm not a girl." She rolled her eyes.

That strange dryness found his throat again. "No, you're not." She was certainly all woman, nothing like the girl he knew when they were teenagers.

"And it's not dating."

His heart fell, though a hitch in her voice suggested less surety than she presented. "I'm not interested in a summer fling," he reminded her as the truck coasted to a stop in front of Wildcrest Wizardry.

They faced each other in their seats. Patty opened her mouth and closed it. Noah waited for her next words, his eyes probing her face for which direction she was leaning. Could he dare hope she was interested in more?

When the silence entered uncomfortable territory, Noah broke it. "Meet me at my parents' house in the morning? I'll confirm a time with them and let you know."

Was it his imagination, or did a flash of disappointment cross her face? It was gone now, if it was ever there.

"Sounds good," she said as she broke eye contact and exited the truck. "See you tomorrow," she called over her shoulder before striding toward Wildcrest Wizardry.

He waited for her to turn back and wave goodbye. She didn't. Frustration blossomed, became another episode of tightness in his chest. He wished he understood what subtext he'd missed in their conversation.

CHAPTER NINE

PATTY

Patty wanted so much to look back at Noah as she walked to the apothecary's door, but she didn't, and she wasn't sure why. Because he'd turned her down again? She wasn't imagining the attraction between them. She knew that.

"Earth to Patty," came a familiar voice, and Patty focused in time to not crash into her older sister, Shelly.

"Hey, sis." Patty grinned at Shelly, who gave her a quick hug.

"Did you just get out of Noah Wright's truck?" Shelly asked, an indecipherable glint in her hazel eyes.

"I did," Patty said. "I went with him to visit one of his patients."

"You don't have to explain anything to me." Shelly opened the store's door, but not before Patty glimpsed her expression.

The merriment was unmistakable. "I'm not explaining anything," Patty disagreed. "I'm…" She stopped herself, unable to find the right word.

"Explaining?" Shelly suggested with a laugh.

Patty half-tackled her sister from behind, Shelly's long black hair tickling Patty's nose. "Whatever. It doesn't mean anything."

At the comment, Shelly pulled from her sister's grasp and faced her. "What does that mean?"

"Do you want a coffee?" Patty asked instead, not meeting her sister's eyes.

"I'll regret it when I try to go to sleep later," Shelly said, "but, of course."

The sisters walked through the apothecary to the coffee shop side of the business, offering a quick wave to the store manager behind the main register. Patty collapsed into one of the wooden chairs, running her hands over the top, hand carved by their Papaw. She'd never tire of seeing his amazing handiwork.

"Hi, girls," Nana greeted them. "Lattes?"

They nodded and watched their grandmother retreat to create the delectable drinks. Nana moved like the former runner she was, her short, wiry frame topped by black, almost spiky hair.

"What's going on?" Shelly asked Patty when their grandmother was out of earshot.

"Why would something be going on?"

"Seriously."

"What?"

"It's been years since I've seen you alone with Noah."

"Wait? What does—"

"And neither of you are teenagers anymore."

Patty's mouth dropped open. "What are you talking about?"

"There's no denying there's something between you."

"I…"

"Everyone could see it at the last festival," Shelly commented offhand.

"Everyone?" Patty squeaked.

"Have you asked him out?"

"Sort of."

Shelly rolled her eyes. "That sounds like the kind of answer I would have given earlier this year."

Patty scrunched up her nose at the thought she was engaging in the same silliness her sister had.

"Either you did or you didn't."

The silence stretched out long enough for Nana to return with their lattes. Her purple eyes narrowed. "Is everything okay?"

"Yes, Nana," they responded in unison, and all three women chuckled.

"Enjoy the coffee."

"We will," the sisters said in unison again.

Shelly inhaled deeply before bringing the piping-hot liquid to her lips.

"Careful," Patty warned.

"It's worth it," her sister said after taking the tiniest of sips.

Patty sipped at her own, the smooth liquid with a hint of chocolate sliding down her throat. She sighed.

"Exactly," Shelly agreed. "Now out with it."

Patty didn't bother to deny or avoid, and laid out the recent encounters with Noah. "What do you think?"

"We'll definitely revisit your idea about Esther," Shelly said, "but let's focus on Noah first." Her voice dropped with the second half of her sentence.

Patty appreciated the effort at discretion, but in a small town, eh, it would be all over Wildcrest by dinnertime that she was hanging out with Noah. "You're not wrong. There's an attraction between us."

"Did he acknowledge that?"

"Not immediately, no."

"What does that mean?"

"I read his aura," Patty admitted.

"Without his permission," Shelly said, the shock clear in her voice.

Patty defended herself. "It flashed so bright the first time, it was impossible to miss." She smirked.

"Okay, fair enough. But be careful," Shelly cautioned her baby sister, before sipping her coffee.

"I am, I promise."

"Then what happened?"

"He said no when I asked him out."

"Really?" Shelly narrowed her eyes. "What aren't you telling me?"

Patty became very interested in the cup of coffee before her on the table. She wrapped her hands around her mug, brought the delectable drink to her lips.

"Patty." The warning tone in Shelly's voice was one only a big sister could use.

"I may have suggested I only wanted a summer fling."

"Ah." Shelly sipped her coffee. "And do you?"

"Want only a summer fling?" Patty drummed her fingers on the wooden top. "I thought so. That made sense. He's hot. I'm cute—"

"If you do say so yourself," Shelly interrupted.

"—but I'm going back to school soon and I just asked his father for a job."

"Wait, what?" Shelly interrupted. "A job?"

"Oh, yeah, I didn't tell you," Patty said. She quickly brought her sister up to speed.

"That sounds amazing. Congrats, sis."

"Elijah hasn't offered me the job yet."

"The one you created?" Shelly scoffed. "He will, you're fantastic."

Patty flushed with pleasure. "Thanks. You can see, right, that in the moment, it seemed too complicated to add a relationship."

"And now?"

"He's not just hot." Patty's eyes took on a faraway look. "He's compassionate, funny, and sweet."

Shelly snorted.

"What?" Patty asked, the spell she'd put herself under broken.

"You surely already knew those things."

"There's a difference between knowing something in the abstract, and seeing it play out in front of you." Patty pursed her lips, remembering her sister's shenanigans from earlier that year. "You, of all people, should understand that." She sipped her coffee, giving her sister a knowing look over the top of the cup.

"True." Shelly blushed. "Now what?"

"Now what, what?"

"Now that you've realized that you want more than a fling, what are you going to do?" Shelly pointed at her sister. "Do I have to spell it out?"

Patty laughed at the unintended pun, and after a moment, Shelly joined her.

"I have a plan," Patty answered her sister.

"Uh-oh." Shelly shook her head. "You know where my planning got me."

"You got the guy!"

"Not for lack of trying to screw that up."

"Do you want to hear my plan or not?" Patty asked.

"Of course."

Patty laid out the idea she'd shared with Noah for helping his mother and impressing his father. "Naturally, the result will also be that Noah will see me as more than just the youngest Newsome—"

"I doubt that's all he sees you as," Shelly interjected.

"—and we can go out on a real date, and maybe have something more after I graduate."

Shelly reached across the table to take her sister's hands in hers. "I think that sounds like a brilliant plan."

"You do?" Patty asked, a shock of surprise hitting her.

"It's much better than my plan had been."

"Any plan is better than your plan was," Patty pointed out.

"Touché." Shelly checked her watch. "I need to pick Ben up. Do you need a ride?"

"I do, thanks."

The women waved goodbye to Nana and headed to Shelly's bright orange VW bug. Patty's mind swirled with the possibilities. It would work. She would help Esther understand and control her magic. That would impress Elijah enough to hire her upon graduation. And, Noah would see what an amazing team they made, not just as friends, but as more.

Tomorrow morning would begin Phase I.

CHAPTER TEN

NOAH

Noah, Ben, and Aaron sat at the kitchen table opposite their parents, who stared at them with curious anticipation.

"You boys called this meeting," Elijah said, his deep baritone rolling around the room. "It looks like something serious. Perhaps you should just say it."

Ben and Aaron glanced at Noah, and he gave a slight nod. "Mom, Dad, we have some… news."

"What is it?" Esther asked, placing her hand over his.

Noah's heart lurched. His gut told him this would ultimately be good news, but it was such a bombshell that he wasn't sure how to introduce the topic. Perhaps his father was right and he should just jump in with it. Or he could work his way toward it. That seemed safer.

"How have you been feeling, Mom?" he asked, covering her hand with his free hand.

She squeezed his hand beneath hers. "I'm fine. Why do you ask?"

Noah exchanged another look with his brothers. "Has anything been different? Felt different recently?"

The skin around his mother's mouth tightened, but she demurred. "Of course not."

When Elijah grimaced, Noah brought in the big guns. "Dad, is that correct?"

Esther rewarded Noah with an irritated sigh. "You don't need to ask your father how I'm doing," she snapped, but appeared contrite. "Sorry about that." Esther pulled her hand from her son and fanned herself. "Maybe I haven't been myself."

"We promise we have a reason for asking," Ben encouraged her.

"We do," Aaron chimed in.

The three men smiled at their mother; her chuckle reduced the tension in the room. "Your father is right. Why don't you just tell us what's going on?" Although her tone remained light-hearted, the flash of worry on her face told Noah that she knew something was awry.

Noah's lips thinned into a line and he blurted out, "You've developed magic."

Elijah's mouth dropped open and Esther belly laughed. "I don't think so," she disagreed.

The doorbell interrupted Noah's intended reply to his mother. "Perfect timing," he said instead.

"Perfect timing?" his mother echoed. "Are you expecting someone?"

"I'll get it," Aaron offered.

Noah thanked his younger brother and stood, preparing to greet their guest. "Patty Newsome is here, and she can explain it much better than I can."

Esther quirked an eyebrow. "Patty can explain what? That I have magic?" She shook her head, her French braid not budging. But her eyes narrowed. She knew Patty's magical inclination.

"Hello Wrights," Patty sang out when she joined them in the kitchen, Aaron a step behind, though he quickly retook his seat at the table. She stopped next to Noah and looked up at him, seeming to search his face for something.

"Hey Patty," he said softly and her grin lifted his spirits. "Are you ready to explain to my mother?" If he wasn't mistaken, her face paled a little at his question.

"You haven't told her?" she hissed, trying to keep the comment between them. "Laura couldn't make it?"

"I was getting there," he said, breaking eye contact. "And, no, she couldn't."

"You know I can hear you both, right?" Esther's fingers tapped on the tabletop. "I'm not even ten feet away."

"Sorry, Mom."

"Sorry, Esther."

Their simultaneous apologies resulted in a shared conspiratorial look. Patty took the seat Noah had vacated. "You're right. We should not have a conversation about you. We should have this conversation with you."

"You know what Noah meant when he said I have magic." A statement, not a question.

Patty nodded. "I do." She brought Esther through the story of seeing Esther's chaotic magical aura at the Lammas celebration; her theory of the magic interfering with Laura's magical abilities; and her offer to help Esther tame the chaos by combining her own magical ability to read auras with Noah's healing. Both Noah's parents' mouths hung open at the end of the tale.

"That does explain a few things," Elijah said, more to himself than anyone in the room, though Esther responded.

"What does it explain?"

Elijah wrapped a hand around his wife's shoulders. "Lately, I can feel a strange pull related to my memory magic. Memories randomly floating to the surface. Other people's memories popping into my head when you and I are with them."

She gasped. "Why didn't you say anything?"

Elijah blushed, a sight so unusual that Noah's eyebrows about jumped off his forehead. "Given some of the, um…"

Now all three sons stared at their father. Elijah Wright speechless? They didn't think it was possible.

"Spit it out, dear," Esther encouraged him with a kiss on the cheek.

"You've been a little moody and seemed to have, maybe, hot flashes," he said in a rush. "I thought it was just, you know, menopause."

Esther sighed. "Well, you're not wrong. That's what I thought too."

"The two may be related," Patty interjected, and everyone looked at her. She waved her hands around for emphasis as she explained. "As we're all aware, magical inclinations appear during puberty. That didn't happen for Esther." She grimaced. "Sorry for the bluntness."

"No need," Esther assured her.

"Why does that happen?" Patty asked, and nobody answered. "That wasn't really rhetorical," she said with a smirk.

Noah snorted and his brothers side-eyed him, which he ignored. "Our best guess is that the inclination appears during puberty because of the hormonal changes..." He trailed off when the implication hit him.

Patty pointed one hand at him and touched her nose with the other. "Bingo."

"It may be menopause that's triggering the magical development," Ben concluded for them and clapped his hands together. Noah almost laughed at the medical scientist in his brother, salivating at this *new witch thing*.

"Has that ever happened before?" Esther asked.

Noah and Patty exchanged glances before she jumped in to answer. "I don't think so, no. I've never come across anything like that in my own magical research."

Patty and the men stared with trepidation at Esther, waiting to see her impression of this development. She broke out in a wide grin.

"That might make going through menopause worth it," she declared. "How are we going to make it work right?"

Noah's worry evaporated at his mother's question. He should have known she'd not only take it in stride, but see it as a blessing from the Goddess. Noah grabbed Patty in a bear hug, which she enthusiastically returned. Her sweet vanilla scent filled his nostrils and he could almost rest his chin on her head.

He barely resisted kissing her, and his heart hammered that she'd gotten under his skin like that. If only she wanted more than a fling. He knew he wanted to date. The temptation of accepting her where she was – offering a fling – surfaced. No, that would only lead to dissatisfaction when he couldn't have more.

She didn't want to date. She'd asked for a fling. That broke the spell, and he held her at arms' length, offering a lop-sided smile, which she matched, confusion mixed with attraction clear on her face.

CHAPTER ELEVEN

PATTY

The unexpected hug threw Patty for a loop. Her body tingled where theirs had touched, a quite pleasant sensation. But she needed to focus on the issue at hand. Helping Esther get a handle on her new magic.

"Have you noticed any abilities that started around the time of menopause?" Patty asked.

Esther tapped her fingers on the table while she thought. "Not that I'm aware of."

"You mean you can't hear animals talking to you?" Aaron joked, and his mother smiled indulgently at him.

Patty ignored him. "Hmm, so either that hasn't manifested yet, or it's something not obvious."

"What does that mean for your plan?" Noah asked.

"Let's try to help the chaos calm down," she said with a quick nod of her head. "Perhaps that's why the magic hasn't manifested yet. The magic is still too chaotic." Her voice dropped as if she was talking to herself. A throat clearing drew her attention back to the family surrounding her.

"What do you need from us?" Ben asked.

"I need everyone but Esther and Noah to clear out," she said. "You're well-meaning, but your energy could mess with what we're trying to do," she added, softening the request.

"Understood," Elijah boomed. "Everyone else out." He kissed Esther on the cheek. "You got this, sweetheart."

"Thanks, honey," she whispered back.

Patty's insides melted a little at the exchange. One day she hoped to have that too.

Chairs pushed back from the table and chatter continued while the men left the room as instructed. A quiet descended when only Patty, Noah, and Esther remained.

"Are you ready?" Patty asked.

Esther chuckled nervously. "As I'll ever be. What do I need to do?"

"Noah, sit next to your mother," Patty instructed. Once they were seated, she sat opposite. "What we're going to do," she reminded Esther, "is combine Noah's healing power with my ability to see your aura to help direct you toward calming and organizing your aura."

Esther squinted. "Yeah, you said that before. Do you have any idea how to do that?"

Patty flushed at the direct question. "Kind of." She pointed at Noah. "I'll need you to verbalize what you're doing with the healing energy. That way I can direct you to push, pull, or otherwise redirect your energy when I see the impact on Esther's magical aura." She opened her arms wide, ignoring the anxiety racing up her spine. "Easy peasy, right?"

"Easy peasy," Esther echoed.

"Let's do it," Noah said.

"First, I'm going to open myself up to seeing your aura, Esther." Patty relaxed and allowed her mind's eye to open. Fuzzy and indistinct at first, a glow took shape around Esther's body. "We're all going to verbalize what we're seeing, doing, and feeling. Right now, I'm seeing a sort of murky white aura surrounding you, Esther."

"Doesn't white signify connection to the Goddess?" Esther asked, her voice trembling.

Patty nodded but frowned. "Except that when it's murky like this, and turbulent, it signifies instability, waiting for a specific change." Her face brightened. "Which makes perfect sense, if you think about it. Your energy is undergoing a significant change right now. It makes sense that your aura reflects that."

"What do you need me to do?" Noah asked, placing one hand over his mother's on the table, to still her nervous tapping.

Esther visibly relaxed at Patty's explanation and her son's touch.

"This is where we're flying by the seat of our pants," Patty admitted. "Noah, I need you to direct your healing energy at your Mom, and do what you do. Think organizing, healing thoughts." She offered a shrug. "Let's see what happens."

Noah faced his mother. Their eyes dilated, possibly with the intensity of the energy exchange.

"Don't forget to verbalize," Patty reminded him.

"Oh, right." Noah closed his eyes for a moment and then reopened them. "I'm asking the Goddess to direct my healing magic to surround my mother." He raised his hands, like he had with Bobby, and moved them over his mother.

Patty's fingers played the air like she was playing the piano. "Ooh, interesting, when your light pink and blue aura mixed with hers, Noah, the colors muddled, and as yours surrounds hers, now fluctuating tán is interspersing with the murky white."

"What does that mean?" Esther asked.

"I have a pink aura?" Noah asked.

"Light pink and blue. That makes sense too," Patty answered Noah first. "Both are common colors for healers, plus pink shows with gentle souls who place great importance on romantic love." Her eyes locked with Noah and a shiver traveled the length of her body.

Patty broke the connection and answered Esther's question, though she swore Noah's eyes remained on her. "Total guess here. If you've always had some kind of latent magic, which seems likely, tan might have been your magical aura color, since it represents the logical, analytical side of you."

"Analytical would be accurate," Esther agreed.

"Guess there's a reason you make a great Chief Financial Officer," Noah added.

"Thanks, son."

"This is good. Please keep going, Noah," Patty instructed, keeping her eyes on Esther's aura.

"Yes, ma'am," he said, offering a mock salute that drew her attention. "I obviously can't see what's happening, Patty, but I can sense something pushing back against the energy I'm floating around Mom."

"Hmm, okay," Patty said, peering at the aural changes. "The tan is… almost pulsing… bigger, then smaller, bigger again… as your energy surrounds her."

"What about the murky white?" Esther asked, her voice tremulous again.

"That's not changing. Which isn't necessarily a bad thing," she rushed to add, seeing Esther's stricken expression. "Remember that you're experiencing something totally unique, to my knowledge. I figured we'd need multiple sessions." She peered back and forth between mother and son. Beads of perspiration dotted Esther's upper lip. "How are you both doing?"

"I can keep going," Noah answered.

Esther remained silent.

"Do you need to stop?" Patty asked gently.

"Let's try one more time." Esther offered a tight smile. "It's hard to describe. It's almost like a tug-of-war. Not just in my mind, but throughout my body. I've never felt anything like it."

"Are you sure you want to keep going?" Noah asked, his brow furrowed with concern.

This time she patted his hand. "Yes, let's try one more time, and then we can stop for the day."

Noah resumed staring into his mother's eyes and lifted his hands. "I'm again directing my energy, through the Goddess, to surround my mother and help her find internal peace, to organize that which is chaotic."

Patty liked the archaic-sounding word choice. "Nice," she whispered.

"What?" Esther asked. The inflection in the single word combined with her rubbing her palms on the table hinted at tension or anxiety from the process.

Patty wanted to reassure Esther that everything was positive. "You're doing great. The tan is receding again, and it's being replaced by streaks of silver through the murky white." She sighed happily at the transformation. Esther's aura was unlike anything Patty had seen before. "It's beautiful."

"Is it okay that the tan is shrinking?" Esther asked.

"I think so." Patty hesitated to offer supposition, but decided she was in the best position to do so. "Another educated guess, but it's almost as if tan isn't the ultimate goal for your organized magical aura, if that makes sense."

"Am I going to lose my analytical mind?" Esther asked and Patty picked up on her half-joking.

"Nah, I don't think so." Patty patted Esther's hand on the table. "Remember that the magical aura represents your magical abilities, for the most part. I mean, it also telegraphs personality and emotions too. Really, it tells the story of who we are." She spread her hands wide. "But mostly it conveys our magical inclinations."

"That clarified everything," Noah said drolly.

Patty winked at him. "I try."

"What about the silver?" Noah asked.

"That could be a number of things," Patty said, as the tan continued to diminish and the silver streaks replaced it within the murky white. "It's connected to intuition, which may be connected to Esther's eventual magical gift."

"That would be lovely," Esther interjected.

Patty raised her eyes to the ceiling. "It also could be related to your… womanly systems."

Esther snorted. "You mean it could be because of the menopause."

Patty lifted one shoulder in a half-shrug. "It's possible." She directed her attention to Noah. "Is the pushback still there?"

"Not as much, no."

"Okay, good." The beads of sweat on Noah's forehead matched his mother's upper lip. "Time to wrap this session up," Patty declared. "Noah, I need you to withdraw your energy, and Esther, tell me how you feel."

"I'm pulling my energy back," Noah said.

"The blue and pink are flowing from your mother back to you," Patty confirmed.

"The tug-of-war in my body is dissipating," Esther said, exhaling loudly.

After Noah's aura settled back around him, Patty turned her full attention to Esther. "The tan is almost entirely gone now. The bit of silver is still there. And although the white continues to be murky, it's not churning as much as it was at the start."

"That's good, right?" Noah asked.

"Is that better?" Esther asked.

Patty nodded in answer to the simultaneous questions. "This was great progress. The colors have changed and the volatility has decreased."

"What happens next?" Esther asked.

"We take it one session at a time. Give it a bit to see how you feel, especially if you notice any… changes of the magical variety."

Esther chuckled. "Understood."

"Everybody good?" At their nods, Patty called out, "Gentlemen, you can return."

Elijah, Ben, and Aaron returned to the kitchen, and Esther, Patty, and Noah gave them the short version of what they'd done and the apparent results.

"That sounds great," Elijah boomed, running a hand through his thick, dark brown hair. "Thank you, Patty, for the suggestion and the progress."

Patty flushed at the praise. "You're welcome, of course."

"If you're done for the day, I'd like to walk you out," Elijah said.

The offer surprised Patty, and her eyes cut to Noah, whose expression reflected the same. That did not go unnoticed by Elijah.

"I have something I'd like to talk to Patty about," he said, offering no further explanation, but excitement fluttered through Patty.

The job offer! Phase I had been a smashing success. Maybe now he'd offer her a job. Her thoughts careened around in her head as she said her goodbyes and followed Elijah to the front door. The two stepped through to the porch and Elijah closed the door behind them.

He turned to her with his hands clasped together at chest height. "Great job you did in there. It sounded like a very positive first step for Esther."

"Thank you." She beamed back at him.

"I'd already been considering your proposal, and this confirmed how invaluable you could be, to the coven and the company."

Patty stayed quiet, though her body trembled inside with excitement.

"I'd like to bring you on, after graduation, as an assistant priestess to start."

Patty gasped. She'd never imagined he'd start her in such a prominent position. The possibility of being just a step away from the high priestess role right after graduation boggled her mind.

Elijah's laughter bounced around the porch. "Yes, I know. It's a big deal. But I believe you'd be great. You are a gifted witch and a forward-thinking businesswoman. What could be better for the role of assistant priestess?"

"Thank you, thank you so much," she stuttered, reaching out a hand to pump his.

His expression clouded. "There's only one condition."

"Name it." There was nothing that would stand in the way of her dream.

"Stop pursuing Noah."

Her mind blanked. She'd surely misheard him. "Come again."

CHAPTER TWELVE

NOAH

Noah's nerves thrummed as he drove his truck to Wildcrest Wizardry to pick up Patty. He'd waited long enough to say his goodbyes to his family, and then called to invite her along when he visited patients again that afternoon. But now, he had the ulterior motive.

Patty lifted her hand in greeting after he'd pulled into a parking spot in front of the building. An uncertain smile flitted across her face, causing his nervousness to skyrocket. She hurried to the passenger side door and, grabbing ahold of the bar assist, hoisted herself into the large truck.

"One of the challenges of being tiny," she quipped.

"You're the perfect size. Snack-sized," he joked back, and a sizzle of attraction electrified the air between them. He hadn't meant the comment like a double entendre. Oh well. Too late now.

Patty focused on buckling her seat belt. "Thank you for inviting me along again. It's great watching you work," she said, changing the subject.

He rolled with the change, thankful for the break from the tension. "Of course. Having your perspective offers a unique opportunity for me to see, so to speak, from the magical side, what's happening."

"Who are we visiting today?"

Noah explained the medical issue of the woman next on his list, cutting his eyes to Patty occasionally. He noted with surprise how she kept her face forward the entire time, nodding at points, but never glancing in his direction, that he witnessed. His explanation ended as they reached the outskirts of town, and he began to turn onto a dirt road.

"Noah, look out!" Patty threw her hands up on the dash and leaned forward.

He slammed on his brakes, even without knowing what caused her outcry. His heart thundered in his chest and he held the steering wheel in a death-grip. His gaze swung wildly to find the source of her distress. There. A desert tortoise languidly crossing the dirt path. Noah had almost hit the large brown reptile.

Both their breathing had become ragged with the near-accident. Now their breath slowed as they watched the tortoise finish crossing.

"Is it okay?" Patty asked.

"I think so," Noah answered. "It's too bad Aaron isn't here to ask." He patted his jeans pocket. "I could always call him to check in with the turtle."

Patty chuckled, the sound strangely nervous to his ears. "It doesn't seem necessary to bring in your family."

The formality of the response sounded even stranger than the chuckle. "Not my family. Aaron." Noah cleared his throat. "Honestly, though, the turtle's moving at a normal pace for his kind, and I don't see any physical wounds." His expression brightened. "I could attempt to heal his energy, just in case, if it would make you feel better."

Patty flushed. "That's unnecessary. You're right. I freaked out a little with almost hitting it."

Now he flushed to match her. This was becoming increasingly awkward. "I'm sorry I was distracted."

She met his gaze full on. "What had you distracted?"

Noah hesitated.

She fiddled with her hands in her lap. "Never mind. I'm sure you were thinking about your patient."

Noah almost took the out she gave him, but remembered his ulterior motive. To work with her again this afternoon, and when they were both relaxed and happy about helping his patient, he'd ask her out.

"Would you like to have dinner with me tonight?" He blurted out the question, kicking himself for veering off the plan.

She grinned for the briefest of moments before her expression clouded.

"I know I said I wasn't interested in a fling—" he said, rushing to fill the silence, assuming he was the cause of her discomfort. His words dried up when Patty placed a hand on his between them on the center console.

"I mangled my invitation before," she said, biting her lower lip before straightening up. "But I'm correcting that now. Yes, I would like to have dinner with you tonight." A shadow again crossed her face, and he wondered at its cause, now that she'd accepted his invitation.

"Are you sure?"

"Yes." She squeezed his hand. "I am."

"We can work out the details after this visit." Joy flooded him at the thought of going on an actual date with Patty.

She faced forward again and, if he wasn't mistaken, her mouth turned down a moment before thinning out.

Noah considered asking her again if she was sure, before realizing this might have nothing to do with him. She'd probably used a lot of energy helping his mother in the morning. The unexplained looks and body language almost certainly were related to that. Patty had done a phenomenal job, but this was all unfamiliar territory to the coven. She'd made her interest in him clear. After all, she'd asked him out first.

Satisfied with this explanation, Noah focused on the path before him and headed toward the next encounter.

CHAPTER THIRTEEN

PATTY

She'd said yes. An actual date with Noah. Not a fling, like she'd said before. Instead of excitement about this step forward, as she prepared for her date, Patty found herself beyond conflicted. The rest of the afternoon with Noah had been better than the awkward conversation in his truck. She could almost see him running through possible explanations for her bizarre behavior, and wondered what had worked to finally relax him. By the time they'd reached his last patient, it was almost as if they hadn't had the verbal exchange at all.

Patty pondered her appearance in the full-length mirror that leaned against her childhood bedroom wall. She wore a bright yellow sundress that skimmed the tops of her knees. Given that she was height-challenged, dresses always were a touch longer than she'd prefer. But the cotton fabric was nice against her skin and she smiled, watching the image in the mirror reflect the same. Her short hair curled around her face and showcased her hazel eyes. She looked good.

"Are you turning into Narcissus?"

She faced the desert owl perched on a sturdy fake tree in a darker corner of the bedroom and mock-frowned. "How is that helpful, Aveline?"

The desert owl hooted again and fluffed her wings. "Ooh, you used my full name."

Patty pursed her lips at her familiar and then shook her head. "Yes, I did, Ave." She'd brought the sandy desert owl up to speed when she'd first arrived home. From working on the chaotic magic with Esther and Noah in the morning to Noah asking her out when they spent the afternoon visiting patients.

"Did Elijah really say owls eat rabbits?" the owl asked.

"I couldn't believe it," Patty said. She paused in rubbing the vanilla lotion onto her arms, her mind flashing back to the morning's conversation with Noah's father at the front door.

After she'd questioned Elijah's proviso, he'd rushed to explain himself...

"I like you," he'd said, taking her hands in his. "You know that."

She'd pulled her hands away, speechless in the face of his request.

"I saw the interest when you and Noah hugged."

"And?" she'd bit out.

"You're not a good fit for my son."

She opened her mouth to question that statement.

"Even your familiars are enemies," he'd quipped.

"What?" Her confusion at that moment had been profound.

"Owls eat rabbits." He'd looked so pleased with himself for the little joke.

She, however, had not been pleased. "I'm going to need a bit more than that."

Elijah had the good grace to appear chagrined.

"Why don't you think Noah and I are a good fit?" She'd gripped the handle of the front door with one hand, the other planted against her hip.

Elijah placed a hand against the door, as well, almost like he was mirroring her. "He's worked to establish his practice and is ready to settle down. You're still in school and preparing to start your career." Now he clasped his hands in front of him.

Patty wanted to shake him from his relaxed stance. "Yes, I'm preparing to start my career. That doesn't mean I'm not ready…" She'd floundered a bit at the end. What *was* she ready for personally?

"I know it seems personal, but it's really not. One day you'll thank me for seeing what you couldn't," he assured her.

The certainty and openness in his tone and expression had flummoxed her. He really thought he was doing the right thing…

Aveline hooted again, bringing Patty back into the bedroom, where she recognized she was playing with fire. She'd accepted the job offer from Elijah, including the one proviso that she not date Noah. Ave, of course, being the nearly eternal being that she was, thought Patty was doing the right thing.

"He means well," the owl said.

"You think so?" Doubt dripped from Patty's voice.

Aveline fluffed her feathers. "I do."

"Then explain it to me like I'm a child. Because all I see is a parent trying to control a grown man," Patty grumbled, sitting on the cheery yellow comforter on her bed. She propped her head with her hands.

"It's like he told you, after the ridiculous thing about your familiars."

Patty could practically hear the eye roll in her familiar's words.

"You and Noah are at different stages in your lives, and you're on separate paths."

"But you support my going out with Noah," Patty interrupted.

"I do. I'm explaining why Elijah thinks he's doing the right thing."

"Oh yeah." Patty collapsed back on the bed, listening to Ave.

"As a father, since he believes you and Elijah aren't right for each other, he's encouraging you not to start down what he sees as a negative path."

Patty bolted upright and jumped from the bed. "You don't think he offered me the job solely to keep me from Noah, do you?" She struggled to keep her voice from breaking.

"I do not."

"Okay, good." She picked a brush off the dark wood dresser and ran it through her hair. The strands fell back into place.

"What's going through your mind right now?"

"It made sense to accept the agreement in that moment. Noah had told me no when I asked him out," she said, more to her reflection than to her familiar. "I didn't have anything to lose, and everything professionally to gain."

Patty met Ave's eyes in the mirror over the dresser and offered a wicked grin. "I'm dating Noah. By the time Elijah figures out what I'm doing, Noah and I will be a couple, and he'll never take the job from me."

Despite the assurance in her voice, the quiver in her belly told Patty she wasn't quite as certain of that outcome as she portrayed.

CHAPTER FOURTEEN

NOAH

"A date, huh?" Ben asked Noah. The three brothers stared at Noah's reflection in the bathroom mirror. "It's about time."

Noah cut his eyes to Ben. "Really?"

"Big brother, we all see the chemistry between you and Patty," Aaron said with a laugh.

"Why so nervous?" Ben asked.

Noah turned from the mirror and his younger brothers followed him through the bedroom to the kitchen. He stopped at the island and leaned against it. "I'm not sure," he admitted.

Ben sat on one of the island stools. "Walk us through it."

"He doesn't want to screw it up," Aaron teased, opening the refrigerator and pulling out a bottle of sparkling water. He grabbed glasses for the three men.

"Will you throw a pod in the machine? I have a late night at the hospital," Ben interjected. "Thanks," he added when Aaron complied.

Noah withstood the desire to roll his eyes at Aaron's comment. "You're not wrong, of course." He frowned. "It's more than that."

Aaron sat beside Ben, and the brothers stared at Noah. "Go on," Ben said.

"I don't remember where I left off with each of you, but she asked me out and I said no because it sounded like she only wanted a summer fling."

"Before she headed back to graduate school, right?" Aaron asked.

The scent of coffee wafted over the men.

"Exactly." Noah sipped from his glass of water and idly wondered if having a coffee would keep him up. "I'm of an age where flings aren't my thing."

Ben snorted. "Of an age? What are you, 50?" He jumped off the stool to grab his mug of coffee.

Noah flushed. "You know what I mean."

"You aren't that old and she's not that young," Aaron reminded him.

"I tutored her in high school," he protested.

"Aren't you over the few years age difference?" Ben asked.

"Yes, I am," Noah said, swigging from his water. "You're right."

"Then what's the problem?" Ben persisted.

Noah laid his hands flat on the quartz counter. "I sensed the attraction you mentioned, and after hanging out with her, decided to see if all she really wanted was a fling."

"That's good," Ben said, confusion in his voice.

"And she confirmed that."

"But…" Aaron said.

"But, after helping Mom with her chaotic magic this morning, something seemed off this afternoon with Patty."

"Could it be she was just magically drained?" Ben asked.

Noah pointed at him. "That's what I thought, too."

"Now you suspect it's something more?" Aaron asked.

"She was quieter all afternoon—"

"Which would happen with an energy drain," Ben interjected.

Noah ran a hand through his thick hair. "It's hard for me to explain. She seemed distant. I noticed she looked… almost sad, a couple of times."

Now Ben frowned. "Yeah, that wouldn't be from an energy drain."

"Did you ask her?" Aaron asked with a shrug. He was always the most direct of the brothers.

Noah flushed again. "Not exactly."

"So, no." Aaron shook his head and sipped some water.

"I double-checked she wasn't having second thoughts about the date."

"And she wasn't?" Ben asked.

"Not that she said." Noah sighed. "I do like her. Once I got past my age hang-up," he added with a half-smile.

"That was silly," Ben helpfully pointed out, and now Noah rolled his eyes.

"What can I say? I'm only human."

"My advice? Go on the date and have a great time." Aaron came around the island to slap his brother on the back. "You two have obvious chemistry. You'll probably find out tonight whether her behavior has anything to do with you."

That was what worried Noah.

CHAPTER FIFTEEN

PATTY

Butterflies actually fluttered in Patty's stomach as she stared at Noah across the table from her. He stunned in dark jeans, a gray button-down top, and a blue sport coat. She felt underdressed in her typical sundress, but if the glint in his eye was any indication, he liked the yellow dress just fine.

"You're beautiful," he blurted out, and relief flooded her at the confirmation. "I should have said that as soon as I saw you."

"Better late than never," she quipped and then cut her eyes away, pretending to take in the décor as if she'd never been to The Cozy Coven before. It was Wildcrest's only

82

upscale restaurant, and where everybody went for first dates and anniversaries. She hadn't been surprised when he'd picked it. Plus, the food was amazing, an eclectic fusion of international cuisines. Even now, the scents of Italian herbs blended with spicy curries. The intoxicating combination made her stomach growl. Her gaze moved between the vaulted ceilings with the wood beams and the other white tablecloth-clad tables in the dining room.

"Good evening. My name is Jackson, and I'll be taking care of you tonight. May I get you something to drink besides water?"

Patty silently thanked the waiter for his appearance, saving her from further awkwardness. "Yes," she rushed to answer, before thinking to ask Noah, "Did you want to share a bottle of wine?"

Noah agreed, and they spent a moment deciding on a nice red, and then Jackson retreated to get the bottle, leaving them to decide on their meals. "When's the last time you were here?"

She wondered if this was his way of asking if she'd been on a date here before, and she bit the inside of her mouth to stop a chuckle from bubbling out. "In all honesty, I haven't been here too many times. I think the last time was when Shelly launched her business."

"It's a great place to celebrate." He sipped his water, his eyes never leaving her face.

She mirrored him and kept chattering. "It is! Shelly was so excited and nervous about branching out on her own. We were so proud of her. She's worked hard to make it a success. Once Shelly finished the coven website redesign, she got more work than she could handle. She's had to turn down work." Patty paused to breathe.

"That's so great for her. Being able to do what you love, and be successful at it, is important."

"That's why I'm excited that I have the job offer from Wildcrest Witches International," she said, and immediately wanted to retract the words.

"What? You got an offer? That's wonderful. Congratulations. I had no doubts," Noah said, reaching a hand forward as if to take hers, but then pulling it back. "You're definitely moving back to Wildcrest after graduation?"

"It looks that way," Patty said. Her tone must have been off because he tilted his head. But he said nothing. She wondered if he suspected she was hiding something. Except since he hadn't known about the job offer, he couldn't know about his father's proviso. If only she hadn't gotten herself in this mess to begin with—wait, she silently argued with herself. This wasn't her fault. Or Noah's for being so attentive, honest, and ruggedly handsome.

"What's the job?" he asked, interrupting her thoughts.

Before Patty could answer, the waiter returned to take their order. "We haven't even looked at the menu yet,"

Patty admitted. She scanned the Thai section. "If you still have the red curry with vegetables, I'll take that." When Jackson confirmed, she handed him her menu.

"I'll have the barbecue chicken platter," Noah added, handing his menu to the waiter as well. "Can't go wrong with good barbecue chicken."

The waiter promised the meals would be out soon and withdrew.

Noah lifted his eyebrows expectantly. "The job offer?"

She flushed. "Right. I'll be your father's assistant," she said, downplaying the offer by not providing the title.

He frowned. "Assistant? With a master's degree? That's not what you proposed to my Dad, is it?"

"Assistant priestess," she clarified, and his eyes widened.

"Now that's different," he exclaimed. "That's amazing."

She nodded, not meeting his eyes.

"Is something wrong? Do you not want the job?"

"Of course, I do. Accepting it is only a formality. It's just… jitters," she stammered.

"You'll do great. You've always been so intuitive—"

"I mean, I read magical auras," she interrupted with a self-deprecating shrug.

"That's not what I mean. Besides your magic. Like the way you're helping my mom. That's more than just your magic at play."

"You think so?" She'd believed it was more than her magical inclination, too. That also played a part in her desire to be the high priestess one day. It thrilled her to hear him express that belief as well.

"I do. First off, you thought of the idea when nobody else did. And, second, you're risking draining yourself to help, which not everyone would do."

His gushing embarrassed her. "It's not that big of a deal."

"Patty, look at me," he said softly.

She did so warily. While she enjoyed his support, not all of her choices were good ones, and the full force of his loyalty and encouragement created an uncomfortable tightness in her chest. She reminded herself she was doing the right thing, not telling Noah about his father's proviso.

"It is a big deal. Family is everything." He reached across the table and took her hands in his.

"Family is everything," she agreed, and her fingers tightened in his as guilt flooded her. No, it would be okay. Elijah would realize it was a mistake when he saw her with Noah. There would never be a risk of a strain in the two men's relationship from the proviso. "I'm glad I can help Esther," she said, focusing on the man before her.

"Me too." His thumb drew circles on her palm and tingles raced up her spine. "I'm glad I got past my hang-ups to ask you out."

"Me too," she agreed, swallowing the desire to blurt out his father's demand. Once Elijah saw how happy she and Noah were together, he'd relent.

Noah's aura flashed bright pink and green.

Patty watched the swirl of colors.

"What happened?" he asked.

"What do you mean?" she asked in response, still distracted by the unexpected flash, though now it faded.

"You're somewhere else."

She put her hands together. "You know I don't read auras without permission, right?"

He nodded.

"But sometimes they appear when there's a strong emotion."

"Ahh," he said. "You're about to apologize for reading my aura without permission."

"Kind of. Though in my defense—"

"You don't need a defense," he assured her. "I guess I can't hide that I'm interested in you."

"Not really," she said.

"What did it look like?"

Relief and joy swirled in her at his quick acceptance of her magical quirk. "It was the prettiest shade of bright pink and green."

"That's an interesting combination, but common with healers, right? Similar to what you saw when we were working with Bobby and my mom."

"Absolutely," she agreed, "and also when you're in love with someone who balances your energy."

His jaw dropped open.

"Oh, my Goddess, I didn't mean… it's probably more…," she stumbled over her lack of an explanation. Did she seriously just use the word *love*? What was wrong with her?

A low laugh rumbled in his throat. "It might be a little early for that, but I guess an aura doesn't lie."

"No, it doesn't," she whispered. They clasped hands again. Tender yearning filled her. She knew this was right. They were right together.

Now she needed Noah's father to accept it.

CHAPTER SIXTEEN

NOAH

Noah thought about Patty the rest of the night, and was still thinking about their date when he knocked on his parents' front door the next morning. It hadn't been a planned visit; his mother asked him to bring a box of books to Ben. There was no rush, but Noah figured, why not do it now before his afternoon patients?

Esther wrapped her arms around Noah and pulled him into the home. "Good morning, honey." She released him and pointed to a box sitting on the dining room table. "That's it. Not too heavy. They're mostly paperbacks. Not hardbacks."

Noah peeked inside and guffawed. "These are Ben's adventure books from when he was a kid. He wants these back?"

"I believe he's planning on donating them. Your father and I are cleaning out the garage," she explained.

"Ah, got it. No problem. I'll throw them in the truck and drop them at the house later."

A booming voice reached them. "Is that my eldest?"

"Yes, Dad. It's me," Noah hollered back. "Mom asked me to bring the books you found in the garage to Ben."

Elijah appeared around a corner and held open his arms. "That's fabulous. One less box in the garage. Your mother has me moving stuff around all over in there."

"It'll be worth it in the end," Esther pointed out as Elijah reached her and looped an arm around her waist.

Noah grinned at his parents.

"What has you all smiles this morning?" his mother asked him playfully.

He didn't even hesitate. "Patty and I went on a date last night."

"You what?" Elijah asked.

"I know, right?" Noah said. "I never would have guessed that would happen. She was always like a little sister to me. Until she grew up."

"That's wonderful, darling. I want to hear all about it," Esther said, leading Noah by the elbow toward the kitchen.

"Of course, Mom." Noah walked with his mother, his father a few steps behind. Once they sat at the kitchen table, Noah summarized his date with Patty. They didn't need all the details.

"She's so sweet," Esther said when Noah finished. "Isn't she, Elijah?"

"She's—"

"Patty told me about the job offer," Noah interrupted his father.

"She did?" Elijah's eyebrows lifted.

"Of course," Noah answered. "Why wouldn't she? She's so excited."

"Is she, now?" Elijah asked drily.

Noah tilted his head. "What's going on, Dad? She's a great fit for the job – and you offered it to her – why wouldn't she be excited?"

Esther joined her son in staring at Elijah, whose expression remained neutral.

"Why wouldn't she be, indeed." Elijah didn't elaborate after his inscrutable comment.

"C'mon," Noah said, "tell us what's going on. What do you know that we don't?" Noah suddenly worried that something had changed between last night and this morning. Had Patty changed her mind about the job?

Elijah stroked his chin but remained quiet.

Noah and Esther continued to stare at him, waiting.

"Perhaps I need to help her retrieve a memory," Elijah mused.

"I don't understand," Noah said. His father's magic was memory magic. He recalled all of his own memories since his magic manifested at puberty and could manipulate energy to retrieve others' forgotten memories, as long as the brain had coded the memory at some point. But Noah couldn't fathom what that had to do with their current conversation about Patty and the assistant priestess job.

"Elijah, quit being obtuse and explain yourself," Esther commanded.

Noah's father steepled his fingers together and looked between his son and his wife. He laid his hands flat on the white oak table and sighed. "I'm surprised to learn that she went on a date with you, son."

Noah furrowed his brows. "I was surprised feelings developed between us, too."

Elijah's eyebrows furrowed in an identical reaction. "That's not quite what I mean."

"What did you mean, then? You're kind of freaking me out here," Noah said.

"What exactly did Patty tell you about my offering her the job?"

This conversation with his father was maddening. "Not much. Just that you'd made the offer and she'll start after she graduates at the end of the year." He squinted at his father. "What are you dancing around?"

"You should call Patty and invite her over," Elijah said instead.

The non sequitur threw Noah. "Not until you explain what's going on," he demanded.

Elijah flushed, a sight which startled Noah and Esther.

"Elijah?" Esther asked.

"I told Patty the job was hers, with one proviso."

"What was that?" Noah asked.

"That she couldn't date you."

CHAPTER SEVENTEEN

PATTY

Noah sounded odd on the phone when he invited her over. Given their date had gone well, Patty wondered if there was a problem with Esther and the chaotic magic. He didn't say when she asked, only repeated the request. Of course, she'd go, but the brick in her stomach became heavier the closer to the Wright home she got.

Patty drove through the wrought-iron gates at the beginning of the driveway. Her mouth became cotton as she parked outside the ranch-style home. Esther surely must be fine. There wasn't a reason for her to have a problem related to the work Patty and Noah had been doing with her. Patty tapped her knuckles on the teal front door.

It flew open, revealing Noah.

Patty's wide smile died on her face. "Is everything okay with Esther?" she blurted out.

"What?" Noah asked, confusion clear.

"You sounded off on the phone. I assumed—"

"Please come in," he interrupted her, his voice clipped. His magical aura flashed a murky red and, without her desiring to, she now had confirmation of Noah's frustration and sadness.

She wrapped a hand around his bicep. Energy radiated off of him.

He didn't quite jerk away, but broke contact and strode toward the kitchen.

The acidic taste of fear burned her throat. Was this an issue with Esther? Or something else?

Esther and Elijah sat rigidly at the white oak kitchen table, their hands mirroring each other as they rested on the surface.

"Good morning, Patty," Esther said softly.

"Good morning, Patty," Elijah echoed in an inflectionless voice.

"What's going on?" Patty whispered her question. "Esther, are you okay?" Another possibility surfaced and Patty squashed it.

In an expression of confusion identical to her son's, Esther paused before shaking her head. "Nothing's changed with me," she answered obliquely.

Patty's head swiveled back to Noah, who stood tall at the side of the table. She found his angry and sad aura overwhelming. Had he found out about the proviso? "Please tell me what's happened," she whispered.

"My father and I talked about the good news of his job offer," Noah said.

The truth of the situation slammed home for Patty, and she swallowed hard. "I can explain," she said in a rush, stepping in his direction, but halting at the swell of his aura.

"Are you reading my aura now too?" he asked, sadness tinged with defeat.

"No," she stammered, "not on purpose. It's just very… prominent." The last word squeaked out.

"Please explain, Patty," Elijah said, his voice quiet but forceful. "I thought we had an understanding."

"An understanding that never should have been made."

The interjection by Noah startled Patty, and she realized that his anger was directed at his father, not her. Patty's arms dropped to her sides, and she rubbed her palms against the cotton of her sundress. "It wasn't like that," she said.

"How was it made?" Noah asked in a level voice that contrasted with his swirling aura.

"You said you didn't want to date me—"

"This is my fault?" Noah quirked an eyebrow.

She flushed. "Of course not. I just meant—"

"And to be accurate, I didn't want a fling."

Patty risked a glance at his parents. Esther's mouth was down-turned and her eyes glistened. With unshed tears? Elijah's face was stonier, but bits of gray shot through his aura, suggesting uncertainty. She wondered if he was regretting his proviso. She certainly regretted agreeing to it.

With a deep inhale, she tried again. "I went into my meeting with Elijah under the belief that there was no future with you."

Noah winced.

"When your father made the offer, then attached the proviso, at that moment, I had everything to gain professionally and nothing to lose personally."

"I can understand that," Noah said, surprising her.

"You can?" Hope bloomed in Patty that they could overcome this horrible situation.

"I can," he said, but his mouth remained a thin line. "What I can't understand is the decision to not tell me."

White hot heat of embarrassment raced through Patty at the comment. "I thought…" She hesitated. "I thought that if we showed your father—" She risked a glance at Elijah, whose expression hadn't changed. "—what a good fit we are, he would change his mind."

A mirthless laugh escaped Noah. "You didn't think I could be part of that plan?"

"I didn't think—"

"No, you didn't," he interrupted her again.

"Please stop interrupting me," she said, "if you want me to answer your questions."

Noah flushed, though at her rebuke, his aura calmed to invisible again. That meant his emotions were calming. She'd only see his aura now with effort, which she wouldn't do. "My apologies." He opened his arms wide. "Please continue."

"I mishandled the situation, I agree." She crossed her arms and then uncrossed them, fidgeting. "I should have told you." She risked another glance at his father. "Part of my thinking was avoiding this scenario."

Noah smirked. "Really?"

"Really," she said. "I know Elijah thinks he's doing what is best, but he's not. The only way I thought to correct this was to keep it from you until he changed his mind. Then it could be something we laughed about later."

Noah's eyes widened. Patty hoped it was at her inference of an ongoing relationship with her.

"I didn't want this," she waved her hand between them, "to cause a rift in your relationship with your father." She offered a crooked smile. "But I also wanted to be with you. That's why I asked you out so awkwardly to begin with."

Noah's stance softened. "I'll have to think about that," he admitted, the hurt in his voice wounding her. "It's hard for me to see past the idea that you didn't feel you could talk to me, or that you didn't want to." He reached out as if to take her hands, then dropped his arms to his sides. "But it's not all your fault." He squared off with his parents, his eyes lasers for his father's.

"Right now, what I mostly see is your betrayal."

CHAPTER EIGHTEEN

NOAH

Noah bit his tongue to keep from commenting about the hard expression on his father's face. Not just because that would be unhelpful, but because he thought he saw something reflecting in his father's eyes. Fear.

"Dad, if we could please chat in the living room," Noah said instead. With a curt nod, his father followed him out of the kitchen, leaving Patty and Esther behind.

Their boots made soft thumps on the red terracotta tiles. Noah stopped beside their white couch but didn't sit. He stared out the window at the expanse of the desert beyond, considering his words.

"Son," Elijah said.

"Yes?"

"I'm just trying to help you." Elijah spread his arms wide.

Noah remained facing the window, considering how to word his response.

"Son?"

The genuine question in the tone softened Noah and he turned to face his father.

"If you could understand what I was trying to do."

Noah quirked an eyebrow. "How is it helpful to give a woman I'm interested in an ultimatum, forcing her to choose between her personal and professional goals?"

"Well, she didn't choose, now did she," Elijah pointed out.

"Don't do that."

"Do what?"

"Lay the blame on Patty for what you started."

"But you told her—"

"How Patty and I choose to move forward is between us," Noah gently corrected his father. "Right now—" He waved his hand between them. "—this. This is between us. Your choice to try to control my life."

"I didn't try to control your life."

Noah raked his hand through his hair and stood even taller. "What would you call it?"

"Looking out for your best interests," Elijah retorted.

"How is that different from trying to control my life?"

His father stepped toward him.

"I'm a grown man." Noah stuffed his hands in his pockets and sighed.

Elijah grasped his son's shoulders. "I know that."

"Then why?"

"She's on a different path than you."

"What does that even mean?" Noah yanked his hands out of his jeans pockets and stepped away from his father. "You know what? It doesn't even matter. This isn't your decision to make, nor your situation to manipulate. Period." He held up a hand to stop his father from interrupting.

Now Elijah crossed his arms, not quite defensive, but getting there.

"I want your word that Patty's job offer has no more strings attached."

"Hmm."

"That's not your word."

"It's important to the coven that our priestess, including an assistant, has her priorities straight." Elijah picked nonexistent lint off his shirt sleeve.

Noah's mouth dropped open. "Are you joking?"

"Whatever do you mean?" Elijah asked.

"Are you really not going to lift the ridiculous proviso on the job offer?" Noah's voice rose in bafflement.

"I'll think about it," Elijah conceded.

Noah stared at his father. This made zero sense. He'd always been stubborn, but this seemed a strange hill to die on.

"If you think you can trust Patty now," Elijah added.

"That's enough." Noah realized the conversation wasn't going anywhere helpful. "Thank you for reconsidering," he stated. "I hope you make the decision that's in the best interests of the family and the coven." With that, Noah strode back toward the kitchen, the silence behind him deafening.

The women met his eyes when he reached the doorway, Esther sad and Patty stricken. His heart sped up at the sight. He couldn't deny feeling rejected by Patty because she agreed to his father's absurd demands and then lied to him about it.

Although technically it was a lie of omission, a tiny voice in his head pointed out. Really, one could argue she got caught in the middle. And she looked miserable. Unlike his recalcitrant father.

Patty approached him, reached for his arm, then let hers drop back to her side. "I'm sorry," she whispered. "This isn't at all what I wanted to happen."

"I know," he said. The tension between them physically hurt.

Patty glanced back at his mother. "Do you still want me to work with Esther, if she still wants me to?" Her hand fluttered at her throat. "I can leave if not."

Her small voice broke his heart, and he took her hands in his. "This issue with my father is separate from helping my mother," he assured her, his heart warmed by the bright smile that blossomed on her face. "I would very much like for you to continue working with her. With us."

"I'm glad," she said.

"Are you okay with doing it now?"

Surprise flitted across her face and she squeezed his hands. "Yes, if she is, absolutely."

CHAPTER NINETEEN

PATTY

Patty acknowledged that none of this had played out the way she'd hoped. She still believed she could make it work. Thank the Goddess that Noah realized she could still help his mother. Patty's goal remained attainable. She would win over both Noah and Elijah by helping Esther. Everyone would let go of the pain and miscommunications. Everyone would have a happily ever after.

She hoped she wasn't being naïve. Maybe she was delusional. But she'd focus on Esther, and the chips would fall where they may. Or whatever the expression was.

Patty sat next to Esther. "Are you ready?"

"I am, if you are," Esther responded, the question in her tone reinforced by a quick squeeze of Patty's hand. Esther's heart was so big, regardless of whatever was happening between her husband and her son.

"I am," Patty assured Esther. "Are you ready?" Patty directed this question at Noah, who nodded and sat opposite Patty and his mother.

"Let's do this," Noah boomed, though the confidence convinced neither woman. So much tension swirled in the room.

Patty took Esther's hands in hers. "Let's start where we stopped before."

Esther nodded.

"Look inside and find the ribbons of magic that have been manifesting," Patty instructed.

Esther's eyes closed and she rested her hands on her legs.

Patty watched the colors swirl around Esther, like before.

"What do you see?" Esther asked.

"It's white with silver streaks," Patty answered. She frowned.

"What?" Noah asked.

Instead of answering, she directed him. "Send your healing energy to your mother."

Noah's mouth thinned into a grim line. "Okay."

Energy swirled around the room, almost a physical presence for Patty. This wasn't going as well as last time.

She gasped as Noah's and Esther's auras tangled together. And they really were tangling. Instead of the light pink representing Noah's intuitive healing guiding Esther's spiritual white, Noah's darker red aura pulsed at Esther's increasingly cloudy aura.

Esther gasped in concert with Patty.

Noah's hands gripped the table. "What's wrong? What happened?"

"This feels off somehow," Esther said, beads of sweat breaking out on her forehead.

Dread filled Patty. Maybe this had been a mistake to try right now. "We should take a break."

"No, I want to move forward," Esther insisted. "It's just a bump in the road."

Patty bit her lower lip. "If you're sure?" Patty wished she had a better sense of manipulating magical auras like this. She didn't believe Esther was in any danger, but she worried that maybe she wouldn't know until it was too late.

"I am."

Esther's determination lifted Patty's spirit. "Noah, I'll need you to take some deep breaths," Patty said.

"Am I the problem?" he asked in response. Guilt telegraphed across his face.

"No." Patty swallowed. "I think it's a mix of all the tension colliding."

"Don't worry, Mom, I can relax." Noah flexed his fingers on the white oak table. He took several deep breaths, as directed by Patty. Nothing happened.

"How are you feeling?" Patty asked Noah, already suspecting the answer.

He flexed his fingers on the table again. "I'm getting there."

Patty worried her anxiety was contributing to the tension issues. She inhaled and exhaled slowly, in tune with Noah's steady breaths. Together, they breathed in concert, and the internal struggle abated for Patty.

The darkness of Noah's aura began to lighten, as well, though it still didn't look as light and lifting as before.

Esther stretched like a contented cat. "That feels better."

Patty watched Esther's aura continue to swirl. It absorbed some of the lighter pink resurfacing in Noah's aura, but the murky white coalesced around the silver and extinguished it. "Hmm."

"Hmm, what?" Esther asked.

"Now it's your turn to relax, Esther," Patty said.

Esther nodded and closed her eyes. Mimicking her son, she breathed in, held it to a four-count, and then exhaled. As with Noah, nothing happened at first.

Patty tapped Noah on the back of his hand. His eyes flew open. "Breathe with her," she mouthed the instruction.

Noah flipped his hand over to squeeze Patty's. They shared the warmth and connection for a moment, before he closed his eyes and joined his mother's rhythm.

Several iterations of mother and son breathing in unison occurred, while Patty tried to ignore how much she missed Noah holding her hand. She gave a silent head shake and focused on the swirling mother and son auras.

"This is looking good," she assured them. Noah's now-lighter-pink aura surrounded and buoyed up Esther's clearer white with the silver streaks. Blips of light yellow appeared, which Patty found curious but not alarming. The color was consistent with Patty's earlier suggestion to Esther that spiritual magic might be Esther's eventual outcome. It also fit with Esther's background as a smart, creative, natural leader. Patty wondered what the actual magical ability would end up being.

"This is nice," Esther said, hugging herself. "It feels… like home. I don't know how else to describe it."

Patty chuckled. "That's a great way to describe it. I think that's what's happening. Noah is helping your magic find its way home."

Noah quirked an eyebrow.

She shrugged. "I don't know how else to describe it, either." A weight lifted. "It's beautiful."

"That's great," Noah said and found Patty's gaze. His smile strengthened and then slipped a fraction.

Would this not be enough? Patty found herself distracted by the tension between herself and Noah. They broke eye contact, stared through the kitchen doorway toward where Elijah had gone, and the damage was done.

"Focus on your mother," Patty directed Noah, hoping to head off where the auras were going, as first Noah's aura darkened with grays of uncertainty, and then the shade found its way to Esther's aura. The white and silver aura became cloudy again, with murky red forming.

Esther glanced between Patty and Noah, her eyes widening. "What's happening? Something has shifted."

Patty wanted to cry, but she needed to focus on salvaging the session for Esther, so she inhaled and exhaled while Noah spoke to Esther.

"It's okay, Mom. Let's just refocus." Noah reached across the table to rest his hand on his mother's.

She yanked her hand back. "No. It's not okay. I can feel all the negativity." Her gaze swung around the room. "I don't understand what's happening. Why your father can't just—" She cut herself off and her hands formed fists. "And you." She glared at her son. "Why do you let your father get under your skin like that?"

Noah and Patty exchanged their own wide-eyed glance.

"Esther, are you okay?" Patty asked, knowing the answer, and dreading her role in the ongoing drama.

"I'm fine. This was a mistake. Until the three of you work through your nonsense, you won't be able to help."

With that pronouncement, Esther jumped to her feet and strode from the kitchen.

"Oh no," Patty mumbled, Esther's murky red and cloudy white aura burned into her magical eye.

"What?" Noah grabbed her hand. "What did you see?"

Patty pulled back, her mouth turning down. "Your mother's aura is too sensitive right now to respond well when we're still… working things out."

"What did you see?" Noah insisted.

Patty described the aura. "She was so close to her spiritual aura solidifying. But, the instant we, um, broke concentration, the immediate impact—" Patty's leg bounced against the floor. "As I said, her aura is too sensitive right now. We're too influential over it."

"Now what do we do?" Noah's voice sounded lost.

She came around the table to sit beside him. She touched his cheek, pleased when he leaned into the touch for a moment. "I saw where her aura might be heading, and it was good. But she's too emotional with us… not getting along." Patty stood and paced to the other side of the room. "We need to resolve what's happening between us and with your father."

"I agree," Noah said. He stood and walked to where Patty was rooted into the ground. He stared down into her eyes.

With everything out in the open, she waited for him to ignore his father's edict and forgive her for not being open with him. Then they could work together as a couple on helping Esther move forward.

Patty placed a hand on his waist.

He stiffened and stepped back.

"I thought you agreed," she said, confused.

"I did… I do."

"Then I don't understand."

"My father is right," Noah said.

"Wait, what?" Patty was certain she'd misunderstood.

CHAPTER TWENTY

NOAH

"My father is right," Noah repeated, straining against the desire to break eye contact with Patty. He'd do this right, no matter how painful. "Mom is struggling because our magic is… misbehaving," he said with a wave of his hand.

"That's not what I said. At all," Patty disagreed.

"Did you see what I did?"

"Of course."

"Mom was doing well and then our negative energy caused her to become frustrated and fail." He blew out a breath. This was much harder than he'd anticipated.

Patty slowly nodded her head. "Exactly. Once we work through our issues and settle things with your father, she'll be good."

"One way to work through our issues is to accept we're not on the same path." He ran his hand through his hair. "It's just like with my brother."

"Which one?"

"Aaron."

Now Patty grinned. "That just proves my point."

"It does?" Noah wondered what he was missing.

"Yes. Aaron and Laura chose their relationship over their misaligning magic."

"They got lucky. Laura was willing to accept the possibility her magic might never be restored. I won't do that to my mother. It's not my choice."

"Okay. Following your convoluted line of reasoning…"

He winced at her word choice.

"It should be Esther's choice, yes?"

Noah frowned. Patty had a point. But, no. The chances of something going wrong were too high. His mother's well-being mattered more than his love life. His heart constricted and he swallowed down the pain.

"I can practically see the wheels turning in your head," Patty said with a sad chuckle. "I'm not getting through to you, am I?"

"Look," he conceded, touching her elbow before pulling away. It wouldn't do to be too familiar with her if they were breaking up. Although, they never started dating. A single date did not a relationship make. "You have a point."

"I'm glad you recognize that."

"But," he stressed. "It's not enough."

"I don't understand. You like me, I like you. Your mother said to work through our issues, including with Elijah. She did not agree with your father that we don't belong together."

"Yes, but—"

"No, but," she interrupted. "I've known your mother my entire life—"

"Me, too." This time he interrupted her, and they shared smiles before replacing them with frowns.

"Do you really think she'd want you to sacrifice your happiness for a theoretical problem her magic might have with our negative energy?" Patty swung her arms out wide in apparent exasperation and then planted her fists on her hips.

She was so cute when she was mad. Wait, he couldn't go down that path. Oh, but he wanted to.

"See," she blurted, pointing at him. "Your aura just flashed pink again."

His face reddened. He hated that her power made him an emotional open book around her.

"I didn't peek on purpose," she assured him. "Your emotions are obviously running hot."

He sighed. "They are." Noah sat at the kitchen table and held his hand out for her to join him. When their fingers intertwined, a bolt of electricity ran through him. Maybe she was right.

"You're considering if I'm right."

"How do you do that? I know that's not visible in my aura."

"No, it's not," she said. Her eyes dropped to their hands resting on the table between them.

"I don't deny I'm interested in you. That ship has sailed." He disentangled his hand and placed it in his lap. "It doesn't change the facts. As long as my father doesn't want us together, there will be friction between the three of us, and that will impact my mother. I can't challenge my father at the risk of harming my mother."

"Even if it's not what she would want."

"You don't know that," he argued, though his heart wasn't in it. Patty was right. His mother said for them to work this out. Esther didn't say she agreed with Elijah. "Except she's an exceptional mother who will always put the needs of her sons over her own. I can't let her. I'd never forgive myself if something happened to her."

A tear escaped Patty's eye and tracked down her face.

Noah wiped it from her cheek. "I'm sorry," he whispered.

"Me too." Patty jumped to her feet and strode halfway to the front door before Noah even reacted. "I'll reach out to Esther about continuing to work with her. Solo," she called over her shoulder, pausing for a moment at the door.

"Okay," he announced into the silence after she quietly closed the door behind her.

CHAPTER TWENTY-ONE

PATTY

"Are you home?" Patty asked her sister over the phone, tears streaming down her face while she drove across town toward Shelly's apartment, hoping she'd be there.

"What happened?" Shelly responded in a sharp tone, the worry clear despite the tinny sound of the mobile.

"I'll tell you when I get there."

"Okay, and yes, I'm home. Drive carefully."

Patty smiled through her tears. The joke was she always drove her bright-red hatchback at precisely the speed limit. She'd never gotten a speeding ticket and, if the rumors that red vehicles drew the attention of cops were true, she didn't want to tempt fate.

Minutes later, she pulled into the parking lot of the apartment complex and parked in front of Shelly's building. Patty bounded up the stairs and rapped on the door.

Shelly opened it on the first knock and gathered Patty into a crushing bear hug.

"I can't breathe, big sis."

Shelly released her and held her at arm's length. "You've been crying." A statement, not a question.

Patty rubbed at her cheek, then glanced around. "I don't need everyone knowing my business."

"Of course not, come in." Shelly held the door and Patty headed straight for the turquoise dinette set off the small galley kitchen. "Wine's on the counter."

Patty glanced at her phone to confirm it was at least noon. She could have a lunch cocktail.

Shelly patted her on the back. "It's five o'clock somewhere."

"True enough." Patty grabbed two glasses and poured them both the red wine. "Out of white?" Shelly preferred white to red.

"Brought it over to Ben's house for dinner the other night," Shelly said.

"Makes sense."

The sisters sat next to each other, their knees almost touching. "Okay, spill," Shelly demanded.

Tears pricked Patty's eyes again and she took a swallow of wine. "Fortification," she said, and Shelly patted her knee.

"What happened?" She asked in a softer tone this time.

"Noah broke up with me."

Her sister's forehead crinkled in surprise. "You were dating?"

A laugh bubbled up. "Fair enough. We went on a date and were exploring the possibility of dating," she amended.

"He changed his mind? Why?"

"Because of his parents." Patty stifled the urge to roll her eyes. It was a childish response, but that's what this whole thing boiled down to. She explained Elijah's ultimatum, Esther's continued chaotic aura, and Noah's choice to stop things now before their misbehaving magic made things worse.

Shelly quirked an eyebrow. "Those Wright men don't make things easy, do they?"

Patty barked another laugh. "No, they don't." Shelly had had her own bumps in the road to happiness with Noah's brother, Ben. "That strengthens my argument."

"How do you mean?"

"He gave the example of Laura's misaligning magic as a reason he couldn't risk his mother's just as it's blossoming."

"Isn't Esther's chaotic magic the reason behind Laura's misaligning magic? So everything will be fine?"

"Exactly."

"Noah didn't buy that argument."

The corners of Patty's mouth dropped and she swigged more wine. "No, he didn't. He believes they got lucky figuring out the issue and solving it. He says he doesn't want to risk it with his mother."

Shelly tsked sympathetically. "That's a bind."

"Right? I can't be mad at him for caring about his mother's well-being. But," she said, and her expression darkened, "this all started because Elijah decided I wasn't good enough for his son."

"Elijah means well," Shelly said, "and that's not what he said."

Patty sighed. "I know." She jumped up, poured herself some water instead of more wine, and headed for a cabinet near the refrigerator. "Chips still in here?"

"Of course."

"Like with Noah, it's hard to fault Elijah for doing what he thinks is right. But, just because I'm a little younger and a little wilder—" She winked at her sister before retaking her seat and placing the chips on the table between them. "—doesn't mean Noah and I can't be a good match."

"No, it doesn't." Shelly chewed and swallowed a chip. She lasered in on Patty. "What are you going to do?"

"I'm still going to work with Esther," Patty asserted.

"Can you do that without Noah?"

Her confidence wavered. "I'm not sure. It helped a lot to see his healing magic, and since we've done it twice, I'm hoping there's some residual healing magic I can help her direct."

Shelly tilted her head. "That sounds difficult."

"What else can I do? I made a promise to help Esther."

"And what about Noah?"

Patty cradled her water glass in both hands. "I still think my plan can work."

"Which one?"

"Smart aleck," Patty said, swatting at her sister.

"In all seriousness, you do?"

Patty set the glass of water on the table, a spark igniting within her. "Yes, I do. Actually, it'll work even better now."

"How so?"

"Noah's objection is less about his father's problem with me and more about his concern for his mother."

Shelly nodded. "If you help Esther, it eliminates the source of his concern."

"Exactly."

"What's the next step?"

Patty fished her phone out of her dress pocket and texted Esther. "I'm going to fix this." She chugged the rest of her glass of water. Her phone dinged an incoming text. "Right now." She stood, and when Shelly did the same, Patty threw her arms around her. "Thanks, sis, for always listening to me work through things."

"Of course, little sister. Good luck."

"Thanks," Patty sang out as she headed to the door, down the stairs, and revved her car's engine. Time to restart the plan. This time, it would work. She was certain.

CHAPTER TWENTY-TWO

NOAH

"Oh," Noah said when he saw Patty standing on his parents' doorstep again. He groaned inwardly at his lack of eloquence. "What are you doing here?"

She smirked at his obvious discomfort. "Thanks for the warm welcome."

He flushed and held the door open. "Apologies. Please come in. What can I help you with?" He gave a slight butler-bow and winked. His reward was her giggle. "Better?"

"Much." She stood inside the doorway, fidgeting.

He withstood the desire to embrace her, his arms longing to wrap themselves around her and hold her close.

After what he'd said this morning and his stance on their relationship possibilities, he surmised it would be unwelcome. Although the glint in her eye made him wonder.

Patty entered the living room and glanced around. "Esther agreed to try another session with me."

"Oh," he repeated. This was going great. Such a scintillating conversation.

"Did you have a stroke?"

He laughed and she visibly relaxed; he guessed her attempt at levity was to reduce the obvious tension between them. "I don't believe I did, but in all seriousness, how are you doing another session?" His brow knitted in confusion. "Did you want me there too?"

"I don't think that's a good idea, given what happened this morning." She sank one hand in her dress pocket and pulled it back out.

Was she nervous? "Will it work without my healing power?"

"I don't know, but Esther's willing to give it a try."

"Good." He stared over her head and snickered.

"What's funny?" She stared at him quizzically.

"I was thinking about how short… I mean, petite… you are." The tips of his ears burned.

Her eyes darted to his ears, and then she was stuffing a smile, too. "All you Wright men are the same."

"Are we now?"

"Your ears turn bright red when you're embarrassed."

"Oh, really."

"I remember Ben's doing that around Shelly all the time. Yours, not as frequent. But, definitely right now." She gave a little finger point to the side of his head.

"Hmm." His conversational skills continued to excel this afternoon.

"This isn't about you," she said.

"I know," he replied, his tone defensive to his own ears.

"You do, huh?" She squinted at him as if trying to read his aura. "I'm not trying to read your aura."

Now his guffaw echoed off the walls and vaulted ceiling of the large space.

"What?" She appeared perplexed.

"How do you do that?"

"Do what?"

"Read my mind."

Now she mimicked his guffaw. "I wouldn't end up in half the situations I do if I could read minds."

"So you say."

"So I say." She broke eye contact.

The awkwardness flooded through him and cotton balls clogged his mouth.

"I know you don't want to see me."

"That's not quite right," he protested.

Patty tilted her head. "You don't want to pursue a romantic relationship," she amended. "In any event, as I said, I'm not here for you. I'm here for your mother."

"Yes, you said," he repeated, finally recognizing why he maintained the asinine conversation. He wanted to keep her with him, however possible.

"I made a promise to help her, so whether or not I lose you and the job, I'm going to do everything in my power to do so."

"We appreciate that." The butterflies in Noah's stomach became angry bees, and he crossed his arms. "I wish none of this had happened this way."

"None of it?"

The wistful tone caught him off guard, and his arms dropped to his side. "Not none of it. Just some of it."

"It's not over 'til it's over," she sang out and winked at him.

He narrowed his eyes at her. "What does that mean?"

"Is Esther ready?" she deflected.

A voice floated in from the other side of the home. "If that's Patty, no reason to give her a hard time. You can send her to the kitchen, Noah."

"I will, Mom," Noah called back, his baritone voice echoing in the room.

Patty pointed past him. "I know the way."

He ushered her through. "Of course." He followed behind her, surprised when he reached the kitchen that his father was there too.

"Patty," Elijah said in greeting.

"Gentlemen," she responded. "I'll need you both to clear the room, so I can work with Esther without... tension." She shrugged on the last word, but Noah understood.

"C'mon Dad, let's go," Noah said, grasping his father's elbow and leading him through the sliding glass doors to the backyard. "Let's give the ladies their space."

"Thank you, Noah," Patty said, her tone formal, but her body language suggesting a good mood. She surely couldn't have gotten over this morning already. His father closing the door behind them spared Noah having to respond.

CHAPTER TWENTY-THREE

PATTY

Patty hadn't lied to Noah when she said she wasn't trying to read his aura. Not exactly. She wasn't trying. But it had practically shouted at her. Then, when they'd entered the kitchen, his father's aura flashed. Although Patty never sought auras without permission, both Noah's and his father's auras were quite talkative.

Noah's flowing healing pink aura was so much stronger than that morning, leaving her wondering how much romantic feelings might be brightening it. Elijah's aura swirled a beautiful blue with lighter streaks suggesting acceptance. That buoyed her some. However, both men also had bits of black floating around, too. Black was often associated with negativity, which worried her. The little bits shrank in comparison to the happier colors as she watched. She wondered if her presence caused the reaction. She almost blurted out the auras' activity before the men left the room. Thank the Goddess she didn't. It wouldn't help, and it wasn't like she could be that precise on the meaning, anyway.

Patty perched on the edge of the seat next to Esther. "Are you ready?"

"I'm sorry I made things worse between you."

Patty waved her hand to dismiss Esther's comment.

The older woman captured Patty's hand in her own. "Don't do that."

"Do what?" Patty whispered the question.

"Act like this isn't a big deal."

Tears flooded Patty's eyes and she blinked them away. "I'm not. Promise. It is a big deal. I want the job Elijah offered. I want Noah." She rolled her shoulders. "But, more than that, right now, I want to help you."

"I know you do."

"Which is why you don't need to apologize. You did nothing wrong."

Esther pursed her lips. "I guess not. It just feels like, if I could get this unexpected magic under control, much of the drama would go away." Now she waved her hand dismissively, though her cheeks flushed.

"This is not your fault," Patty said. "Do you understand how rare and amazing you are?"

Esther shook her head. "I'm pretty self-confident, but I wouldn't go quite that far."

"You're the first person any of us has ever heard of to develop magic later in life," Patty enthused. "It's incredible."

"I got old, you mean," Esther responded, but with a light tone.

"I can only hope I'm as exceptional when I'm 'old' like you," Patty said, using air quotes.

"Of course, I don't actually have any magical abilities yet. Just the chaotic aura." Esther shrugged. "You believe the magic will manifest once the aura is under control?"

"I do, but I literally have zero to base that on, except my intuition." Patty's chest tightened at the idea she might be leading Esther on, getting her hopes up for something she'd never get. But Patty believed she was right about the aura and Esther's magic. She grabbed hold of that thought. "You're the one that has to do the hard work," she teased.

"I'm still game." Esther sipped from a glass of tea on the table. "Can you do this without Noah?"

"That I'm less sure of. I saw how close you were before…" She trailed off.

"I went magically nuclear?" Esther offered.

"It wasn't that bad," Patty countered. "There is such a thing as residual magic, so that's what I'm relying on here."

"Noah's magic might still be attached to my aura somewhere?" Esther's uncertainty shone through her words.

"That's the idea. Are you ready to get started?"

"Let's do this."

Patty guided Esther to focus on her inner energy and healing thoughts. A slight smile rose on Esther's face, reassuring Patty that they were on the right path. "This is great, Esther." The aura had bloomed the murkier white like at the end of the morning's session, but now it brightened.

"Think of yourself as connected to the world, to all the living beings within," Patty instructed.

"That feels nice," Esther murmured, her aura lightening further.

"I'm seeing those silver streaks and even the little bit of yellow like before."

"That's good?" Esther asked.

"Yes," Patty answered, concerned that the lightly asked question might mask more self-doubt.

"Okay, good."

Despite the positive statement, Esther's aura darkened. The silver streaks faded. "What are you thinking right now?"

"I'm… not."

"Esther, you need to tell me the truth." Patty straightened in alarm at the spreading darkness of the yellow in the aura.

"I'm worried," Esther admitted. Her hands clenched and unclenched in her lap.

Patty's hands closed over them. She dropped her voice lower, soothing. "Clearing your mind isn't the goal. Think about the connection to the world around you," she said again. "You are a bright shining light within it, whatever your ultimate magical ability may turn out to be."

Esther's aura brightened and then immediately darkened.

"Esther?"

"If I develop my magical ability."

Alarm bells rang loudly in Patty's head now. "Of course, you will. Why wouldn't you?"

"I… don't know." A tear slid down Esther's cheek.

"Would the Goddess gift you a magical aura without a magical ability to go with it?" Patty asked, trying for a joking tone to relieve the tension. It didn't work.

"Why would the Goddess give me a chaotic aura?"

"I don't know," Patty said, echoing Esther's earlier statement. "But." She stopped and stared, bringing Esther's wavering gaze to her own. "The Goddess doesn't do things without a reason. You won't find your reason until you learn to control your aura."

Esther yanked her hands free and stood from the table, though she leaned forward and braced herself against it.

"Are you okay?" Patty rubbed her back in circles.

Esther stood tall, pushed back a stray hair that escaped from her French braid. "I will be."

"Are you sure?" Patty asked. Esther's dark yellow aura screamed self-criticism, so Patty doubted Esther's answer.

"I'm okay," she insisted. "But we can't work on this until you, Noah, and Elijah figure out what to do."

Patty nodded, unsure what to say. Esther's aura was changing, despite what had happened. The yellow was brightening again to a healthier, supportive light yellow.

"It's an odd sensation," Esther continued, her eyes almost dreamy. "I know without question that I can't move forward until you three fix this. But I can't say exactly how I know that."

Patty tasted acrid fear, but a small part of her wondered if this was part of Esther's blossoming magical ability.

"I'm sorry, dear, that sounds terribly self-important. And I don't want to put any pressure on you."

"We've put all the pressure on ourselves, no doubt," Patty said. "We'll work it out." If only she had an idea how to do it. She was in a classic chicken or egg situation. The need to help Esther to remove that barrier to a relationship with Noah and convince Elijah to confirm the job offer. But now Esther was telling Patty that she needed those things to happen before Esther could move forward. *Gah!*

CHAPTER TWENTY-FOUR

NOAH

Noah and his father sat on side-by-side deck chairs. The silence weighed heavy. A slight growl drew both men's attention.

"It's okay, Richard," Elijah said to the gray wolf that had joined them and padded between their chairs on the deck. The wolf shook his head back and forth, his green eyes thoughtful yet alert.

"No, really, it is," Noah assured him, assuming the wolf would remain on alert until the tension between the men lessened. That was probably a holdover from the wolf's warrior days as a human.

Richard settled between them, dropping his head between his paws and letting out a harrumph that sounded human. The laughter it elicited from Noah and his father thawed the icy tension a little.

"Son."

"Father."

They shifted in their seats simultaneously, alike in so many ways. Noah had his father's striking looks and booming baritone. He hoped he wasn't as stubborn as the old man.

"Your proviso was asinine," Noah began.

"No."

Noah quirked an eyebrow at the absolute answer from Elijah, though he wasn't surprised. "That gives us nowhere to start."

"There's no starting here."

"There's not? Then you lied to Richard."

At his name, the gray wolf lifted his head and growled again.

"I did not," Elijah disagreed.

"You told him everything was okay,"

"So did you."

"Yes, because I hoped you would be an adult about this." Noah winced even as the words left his mouth.

The stony expression on Elijah's face confirmed the mistake. "I'm not an adult?"

"That's not what I meant."

"Then tell me what you meant, son," Elijah said in a flat tone.

Noah tapped his foot. "I thought you'd be open to discussing the realities of the situation."

"What are those realities?"

"I like Patty and I want to be with her." The words slipped out so easily and quickly that Noah knew they were unstoppable.

"Indeed."

"And she's a superb choice for the assistant priestess position."

"Hmm."

"You know she is, or you wouldn't have offered it to her to begin with," Noah pointed out. "I don't believe for a moment you offered it to her specifically to convince her to stay away from me."

"Thank you for that." Elijah's softer tone still boomed around the backyard.

"You love the coven and want what's best for us."

"I do."

"And you think you're doing the right thing, trying to keep us apart, but you're not."

"She's young and still finding herself. You're ready to settle down."

"You act like I'm done living," Noah said with a snort.

"That's not what settling down is," Elijah said. "Do your mother and I look like we're done living?"

"Of course not." Noah groaned and realized what his father was saying about his stage in life. "That's where you're wrong, though."

"That your mother and I aren't done living?"

Noah laughed. "No, that Patty's young and still finding herself."

"She's not?"

"Dad, she's only four years younger than me." Noah could smack himself for thinking the same thing as his father in the beginning, that Patty was too young for him. It wasn't that far-fetched for his father to erroneously believe it too. "You also wouldn't have offered her the position if she was still finding herself."

"That may not be true. She's young and impressionable."

With a shock, Noah identified the reason behind his father's contradictory notion that Patty was young and impressionable, yet still the choice for Elijah's eventual replacement. "You wanted to create a mini-you?"

His father shocked him by reddening. "Maybe a little."

"That would never happen."

"I've accepted that Patty isn't nearly as impressionable as I'd thought. She is, however, even more capable."

"You're leaving the offer on the table?"

Elijah lifted his hands in surrender. "Yes, yes."

"Without the asinine proviso?" Noah deliberately left the word in there.

"Your mother told me the two of you weren't seeing each other anymore, anyway," Elijah said, sidestepping the question.

"When I saw Mom in pain…"

Elijah's hands tightened on the chair's sides. "Seeing my love like that.."

"No," Noah agreed. "I didn't want to be the source of that."

"Of course not."

"Much like you, though, with the asinine proviso." He didn't enjoy the discomfort his repeated use of the word caused his father, but the proviso had started a damaging series of unfortunate decisions. The magnitude of the fact needed to be recognized. Then he softened. "Like you, too, I'm a big enough man to admit when I was wrong."

"I never said I was wrong."

Noah side-eyed his father, who lifted his hands in surrender again.

"Fine. I was wrong."

"As was I with Patty. I made a mistake, but I'm going to fix it as soon as they finish this session." He stood suddenly, startling Elijah and Richard. "What am I doing? I should be in there helping Patty and Esther. Now that we've cleared the air and we're on the same page?"

"Yes," Elijah said. He joined his son, and they approached the sliding glass door.

"Something's wrong," Noah said. His mother braced herself against the white oak kitchen table. He opened the door and watched Patty comforting Esther. He waited until a small smile crossed his mother's face, and he knew she was okay, then he entered the kitchen to both fix his mistake with Patty and help his mother.

CHAPTER TWENTY-FIVE

PATTY

The sliding glass door opening drew Patty's attention. The smiles on both Noah's and Elijah's faces heartened her. She rushed to Noah, certain that they were meant to be together. "I'm so sorry," she blurted out.

"I need to apologize," Noah said simultaneously.

They both laughed.

"You go first," Noah said.

"Esther, could I talk to you in the living room?" Elijah asked. Esther took the hint and Noah's parents started to leave the room.

"Wait, Mom, you're okay, right?" Noah asked.

"Yes, honey, I am," Esther confirmed.

"Okay, good. I'd like you both to stay. You should hear some of this, too." His parents returned to sit at the kitchen table, and Noah grasped Patty's hands.

"I'm so sorry," she repeated. "Your father never should have made the proviso. But I never should have accepted it."

"You wouldn't have taken the job? Even though we weren't together?"

"No. On principle alone, I should have rejected his attempt to control me. The job enticed me, obviously, but no job is worth sacrificing your self-respect." At a sound from Elijah, she shot him a be-quiet look. "I'm not finished. I know that's not what your father was trying to do, but it's what in-effect he did." She placed her hand on Noah's chest.

Noah clasped her hand and brought it to his lips.

When he kissed her palm, a shiver of pleasure moved through her.

"I agree with all of that. My father meant well, but his belief that you and I were wrong for each other blinded him. He'll apologize later."

"Thanks for taking care of that for me, son," a sardonic voice interrupted from the table.

A low laugh rose in Patty's throat. "There was enough stupidity to go around."

"Indeed. My stupidity was in blaming you for not telling me about what my father did."

"No," she shook her head. "I should have. We're friends, and his proviso impacted us both."

"From that standpoint, yeah, I suppose. But how do you tell someone your father made an unacceptable proposal?" His eyebrows raised with the question.

"I want to officially date you," Patty said. "If you'll have me." She grinned impishly.

"What about school?"

"We can date until I leave for the fall. We'll have to stay long-distance until after graduation—" She side-eyed Elijah.

"You don't even need to ask. The job will be waiting for you when you get home," Elijah assured her, his voice gruff.

"I'm all in," Noah said, and Patty's heart soared. "Now that's out of the way, are you ready to help my mom?"

The couple faced Esther at the table. She gave an uncertain nod. "I'm ready if you are."

Patty and Elijah sat across from Noah and Esther.

Patty glanced between Esther and Noah. "You two know the drill. Noah, direct your healing energy at your mother. Esther, accept the healing energy of the universe and try to find the center of your developing magic. Our goal is to finish calming the chaos so your magical ability can manifest, your magic won't interfere with others, and maybe your menopause will improve." She threw in the last item as an added incentive to also break some of the nervousness she saw on Esther's face.

"That's all?" Esther asked, quirking an eyebrow.

Noah held his mother's hands and began talking through his internal actions. "Mom. I'm sending my energy to connect with yours."

As before, Noah's aura glowed, this time a gorgeous shade of healing pink. It mixed with Esther's murky yellow and white, which almost immediately lightened. When Patty relayed that information, the remaining tension drained from everyone's faces.

"Let's keep going," Patty encouraged them. "Esther, how are you feeling?"

"Light, almost like I'm floating. Everything feels positive, good." A blush of health rose on her cheeks.

"Your aura is continuing to transform," Patty relayed. "The yellow is growing stronger, but it's a sunny yellow, tied to intelligence—"

"That definitely fits," Elijah boomed.

"Shh, honey," Esther chided him.

"It also suggests creativity and a supportive nature. All of which fits your personality."

"What happened with the white?" Noah asked.

"Focus," Patty said, thinking just how much he was like his father. "The white is still there, but it's also transforming." She watched as rays of light formed; that usually signaled a connection to the higher self and the

Goddess Herself. The glow almost became too bright, it was so beautiful. As she shared that with the Wrights, Patty wondered just what magic Esther would manifest. It would no doubt be as unique and as beautiful as her aura.

Patty sighed happily. "We're almost there. Esther, your aura is so calm, you must sense that."

"I do. I've never experienced anything like this before. Is this what having magic is like?" she asked.

"Maybe?" Patty answered. "Everyone experiences it differently." She placed a hand on Noah's arm across the table. "You can start withdrawing your healing energy now. Do you feel the improved health in your mom's energy?"

His eyes shone with gratitude. "I do," he whispered.

"It's too early for 'I do's'," Elijah grumbled.

Patty ignored him. "Maybe one day," she whispered back to Noah, who curled his fingers around hers.

"One day," he agreed, and pulled her across the table to capture her lips with his.

On the tips of her toes, she used her hands to hold herself above the table, while she enjoyed the gentle pressure and sweet taste of Noah's kiss. They'd made it to their happily ever after.

EPILOGUE

NOAH

Noah watched from the corner of his eye as Patty spoke, resplendent in a purple dress with cartoon black cats on it. She had debated wearing the dress all week, bringing it up every time they video chatted, until she decided that this was her personality. The coven knew her, and they would accept it. And they did, of course. She'd come home from college for the weekend to lead the coven's Samhain celebration. Her job as assistant priestess wouldn't officially start until December, but his father had suggested she lead the ceremony. This would introduce Patty to the coven in her soon-to-be new role.

Patty stood in their coven circle, surrounded by their family and friends, in his parents' backyard. She would lead them through the Summer's End ritual, honoring those who had crossed over the veil, as well as celebrating members' hopes for their new year. As always with their sabbats, folding tables laden with food filled the expansive space outside the circle. Every member of the coven brought a dish that held special meaning for them, representing a lost loved one. In the evening's dusk, the scents of everything from macaroni and cheese to apple pie wafted over the witches.

Members of the circle had already called in the four elements of earth, wind, water, and fire. Although not always included in their rituals, Patty had also called a fifth element of spirit, since tonight the veil between worlds would be at its thinnest.

Noah squeezed Patty's hand in support and she flashed him a quick smile, eyes shining, before focusing on the circle.

"I ask for any of us who have lost a loved one over the past year, if you'd like to speak," Patty said. Her gaze traveled from person to person around the circle. They'd invited several solo practitioners to join them, so the group might have been thirty people strong.

A thin, older man stepped forward. "I'd like to remember my wife, Alyssa." The group listened in rapt attention as he described his thirty-year marriage and her recent passing.

Since they were a small town, even with adding the solo practitioners, the celebration advanced quickly to the witches' plans for the future. Several members of his and Patty's families had looked ready to burst, so he had an idea that they would have a few memorable announcements.

He wasn't wrong.

Patty asked the assembled circle if they had expectations for the next year. His brother, Ben, and Patty's sister, Shelly, exchanged a quick glance and said in unison, "We have an announcement."

"You're not pregnant, are you?" Grace Newsome asked in her husky voice. All eyes swung to the thin, petite woman. Patty's mother threw her head back and howled with laughter, her curly red hair bouncing around her face. Then she winked a purple eye, and added, "I'm just being a smart aleck."

"Thanks for trying to steal our thunder," Shelly joked before she glanced again at Ben. "We're getting married!" they shouted simultaneously.

Congratulations rang out at the news, and Patty jumped in. "This is only the first announcement, everyone. Let's try to stay calm." At her direction, the chatter dropped.

"I'm thankful for my new magic," Esther jumped in next, "and I look forward to continuing to hone it over the next year." She clasped her hands in front of her chest before retaking Elijah's and Aaron's hands on either side of her. "And, in honor of this news, I'd like to offer as my wedding gift, fixing Shelly's misfiring magic." Gasps greeted her offer.

"Great. What am I supposed to get them?" Elijah grumbled good-naturedly.

"We all know I was responsible for Laura's magic misaligning with Aaron's," Esther continued as if her husband hadn't interrupted. "It occurred to me that since my magic is a connection to the divine, including a connection to the organizing energy of the universe, that I can help disorganized magic." She nodded at Shelly. "I believe I can heal your magic, too."

"That would be amazing," Shelly said, her voice thick with emotion.

A high-pitched whistle sounded from a tall tree about twenty feet from the circle. Noah stared at it, but in the dark could not see his mother's familiar perched there. Evelyn, a magnificent bald eagle, had appeared when his mother's magic manifested. Evelyn told the family she was a distant cousin from the 1950s but had been a devout believer, and they figured this was why she'd returned as his mother's familiar.

"Since we're announcing relationship goals," Aaron said, his deep voice rising above the hubbub, which quieted the circle. He locked eyes with his girlfriend, Laura, the redhead stunning as always in what Noah had been told was a designer pantsuit.

"Aaron is moving in with me," Laura interjected with a happy squeal.

"Into the house I helped her find," Aaron added.

The members of the circle maintained their contact, but lifted their hands in support for the happy couple.

After much fast and furious sharing by other members of the circle, the tempo slowed and Patty opened her mouth, possibly to thank them and close the circle.

"I have one more announcement," Elijah boomed into the night. All eyes zoomed to him. "For those of you who weren't aware, Patricia Newsome performed this evening's ceremony at my request. I've offered her the role of the assistant priestess once she graduates with her master's degree in two months. My intention was for her to become the high priestess upon my retirement."

Another lifting of conjoined hands in support of Patty followed. Noah's heart swelled with pride for his girlfriend.

"However," Elijah continued, "recent events have caused me to reevaluate my commitments. More details will be forthcoming, but I plan to go to half-time when Patty graduates, with full retirement by this time next year." Gasps greeted this statement.

"That's unexpected," Patty murmured.

Noah heard the anxiety in her voice.

"And terrifying," she added, confirming his guess.

"You've got this," Noah assured her, squeezing her hand. "Plus you'll have my family and yours there to help, every step of the way."

Elijah kissed his wife's forehead. "I plan to spend all my time with my wife, Esther. At least until she gets tired of me."

"Never," Esther said, wrapping one arm around Elijah's waist and leaning into him.

"Aw, that's sweet," Patty whispered, more for Noah's ears than for the circle.

Understanding dawned for Noah. His father was stepping back to be there for his mother with both the magical manifestation and menopause.

Noah squeezed Patty's hand again. His parents' love never ceased to surprise and warm him. Now, his brothers were moving forward with their happily ever afters. Noah leaned down so that his mouth was at Patty's ear. "We're definitely next," he whispered. Patty's head turned, and she kissed both his cheeks before placing the sweetest kiss on his lips.

"Absolutely," she breathed.

THANK YOU!

Thank you so much for supporting my work and reading this book.

If you liked the book, please consider leaving a review online.

Just a few lines would be great. Reviews are not only the highest compliment you can pay to an author, they also help other readers discover and make more informed choices about purchasing books in a crowded online space. Thank you so much in advance.

If you didn't like the book or have concerns, please email me directly at
heather@heathersilvio.com

ABOUT THE AUTHOR

Heather Silvio mostly writes fun, flirty, fantasy romance and mystery with guaranteed happily ever afters. She sometimes strays from that to write non-supernatural fiction, and even the occasional nonfiction book. Heather is also an actress and clinical psychologist who channels her inner flapper as a 1920s jazz and blues singer when she isn't working.

Visit https://www.heathersilvio.com for more information and to sign up for her Theatrical Thursdays Newsletter.